"DANCE WITH ME," THE NINJA SAID. LEILA COULDN'T hear him over the music, she could only read his lips.

She shook her head. Who was he? She couldn't identify him with that costume on. But he wouldn't take no for an answer. He took her hand and led her to the crowded dance floor. Then he pulled her close, holding her against him with a familiarity that was baffling.

"Do I know you?" she whispered into his ear.

But he didn't answer her. He only held her closer, tightening his arm around her waist until she was pressed fully against him.

"Fifteen seconds to the new year!" a voice shouted, and Leila lifted her head as the crowd around them joined in with the countdown.

"Ten, nine, eight, seven . . ."

The ninja was watching her, and she stared into his eyes, trying to guess their color in the dimness.

Hot. Whatever color they were, they were hot. He wanted her—as if she didn't already know that from the intimate position of their bodies.

"Four, three, two, one! Happy New Year!" "Auld Lang Syne" blared from the loudspeakers.

"Happy New Year," the ninja soundlessly said to Leila.

And then he kissed her.

WHAT ARE *LOVESWEPT* ROMANCES?

They are stories of true romance and touching emotion. We believe those two very important ingredients are constants in our highly sensual and very believable stories in the LOVESWEPT line. Our goal is to give you, the reader, stories of consistently high quality that may sometimes make you laugh, sometimes make you cry, but are always fresh and creative and contain many delightful surprises within their pages.

Most romance fans read an enormous number of books. Those they truly love, they keep. Others may be traded with friends and soon forgotten. We hope that each LOVESWEPT romance will be a treasure—a "keeper." We will always try to publish

LOVE STORIES YOU'LL NEVER FORGET
BY AUTHORS YOU'LL ALWAYS REMEMBER

The Editors

Loveswept ® 787

KISS AND TELL

SUZANNE BROCKMANN

BANTAM BOOKS

NEW YORK · TORONTO · LONDON · SYDNEY · AUCKLAND

KISS AND TELL

A Bantam Book / May 1996

ISBN 0-553-44547-2

Published simultaneously in the United States and Canada

PRINTED IN THE UNITED STATES OF AMERICA

OPM   0 9 8 7 6 5 4 3 2 1

DEDICATION

To Deede Bergeron—for both your
idea and your friendship.
This one's officially for you, but really,
they *all* are.

ONE

Leila Hunt stared into the mirror at the bottom of the staircase, and Cinderella did *not* stare back. And that was a shame, since Leila was dressed just like Cinderella—from the golden hairpiece that matched her own short, blond curls to the glittering off-white ball gown that hugged her tall, slender figure, all the way down to the delicate glass slippers on her feet. Well, they were plastic slippers, really. But like the real Cinderella's slippers, they fit Leila perfectly.

Regardless of all that, Leila didn't look like Cinderella. She looked at herself critically in the mirror, wondering why exactly that was.

Maybe it was because she didn't look as elegant as a fairy-tale princess should. Her face was a little too cute, a little too heart-shaped. Her nose was upturned at the end, and her chin was a shade too pointy, making her look elfin. No, strike that. She was much too tall to be elfin. Elfin implied petite, and at five feet ten inches, Leila hadn't been petite since she was an infant.

What she looked was perky.

God, Leila hated that word.

She stepped closer to the mirror and tried to look sexy instead. She tried to look as if she were keeping some incredible secret. She tried to smile mysteriously, moving her lips only slightly upward.

The smile only made her look mischievous. Perkily mischievous—more like Peter Pan than a princess.

Leila turned from the mirror with a sigh. She still wasn't sure why she'd bothered to leave New York City after Elliot called her at the airport and told her he wouldn't be able to catch the flight to Florida.

Yet here she was, back on Sunrise Key, her hometown, dressed as Cinderella, as if she hoped that somewhere out in the yard, on her brother Simon's rented dance floor, Prince Charming was waiting for her.

She looked around the room. A Batman and a clown lingered in the corner. King Henry VIII, turkey drumstick in hand, sat next to a wizard. There was nary a Prince Charming in sight.

Leila went out the french doors and into the backyard where most of Simon's guests were dancing under a tent to taped music that was blaring out of four sets of gigantic speakers.

"You look beautiful," a voice beside her shouted to be heard over the music. "That dress suits you."

Leila would have recognized that crisp English accent anywhere. It was Marshall Devlin. *Dr.* Marshall Devlin. Dr. Marshall High-and-Mighty, Better-than-Thou, Best-Friends-with-Her-at-Times-Equally-Annoying-Brother, English-Accent-Encrusted Devlin.

Six years older than Leila, Marsh had spent summers and school vacations on Sunrise Key starting when he was in high school. Despite his traditional Englishman's coolness and the short duration of his visits, Marsh and Simon had hit it off immediately. They stayed friends through the years, united in their single goal—or so it had seemed to Leila at the time—either to torment and thoroughly embarrass or to totally ignore Simon's little sister. Namely Leila.

It seemed hard to believe that Marsh Devlin could have been such good friends with one Hunt and such bitter enemies with another Hunt—again, namely Leila. Well, bitter enemies was perhaps too strong a phrase. But Marsh and Leila *had* been adversaries from the word go. Even now that they'd supposedly grown up and become mature adults, they still argued incessantly. Of course, now it was called debating or discussing a difference of opinion. But Leila knew better. She knew that Marsh still kept score.

Out of all of Simon's friends, Marshall Devlin was the one who had the power to infuriate Leila. Out of all of Simon's friends, Marsh was the one who had moved to Sunrise Key, to *her* hometown, and now lived here year-round as the island's only medical doctor.

Out of all of Simon's friends, Marsh also happened to be far and away the best looking. He wasn't handsome in the traditional sense. His face was slightly too lean, too angular. But his nose was impossibly straight and his cheekbones exotically high. His eyes seemed an unremarkable shade of brown until examined from a close proximity. Then they became a swirl of colors—different subtle shades of lighter and darker browns, flecked with greens and even yellows. Marsh was, like his eyes, quietly, subtly gorgeous.

"Poor Cinderella," Marshall Devlin continued as Leila gazed at him. "Have you lost your Prince Charming?"

"Actually, I have." Leila stepped away from the dance floor, away from the pounding music. She kept her voice cool and polite, hiding the familiar surge of adrenaline that seemed to be released into her system whenever she came face-to-face with this man. Her heart gave a little skip that she told herself had to be from jet lag. "Elliot was detained. He won't be here until tomorrow evening."

"Elliot?" Marsh said, a frown marring his lean features. "Ah. Your gentleman friend. That's right. Simon said he was coming for the weekend. What a shame he couldn't be here. New Year's Eve is hardly the time to be by oneself."

No kidding. But truth be told, New Year's Eve was hardly the time to be with Elliot.

Leila had been dating Elliot for the past year. She liked him. They were friends. But as far as romance went, they weren't about to set the world ablaze. Except Elliot had recently started talking about marriage.

Was Leila willing to settle for a life with a man she didn't love? That was the million dollar question. And if she *weren't* willing to settle, was she willing to risk never finding anyone to share her life with? Because, face it, romance took time. And with her crazy work schedule, time was something she didn't have a lot of. She knew she and Elliot were compatible. So, okay, her life wouldn't be filled with hot, steamy, passionate nights, but neither would she be alone.

Except here she was, on Sunrise Key, at the start of her two-week vacation, alone.

It wasn't the first time Elliot had postponed a trip.

And with his schedule, it certainly wouldn't be the last.

With very little imagination, Leila could project herself into the future, to that mystical world of Little League games and dance recitals and chorus concerts and science fairs. She could picture Elliot missing every single one—calling in his apologies to their children over his cellular phone. That would really, *really* stink.

But at least there would be children. Provided Elliot could find the time in his busy schedule to procreate.

"Quite a crowd this year," Marsh said, and looking over the array of costumed guests, Leila had to agree. Simon's guest list must have included nearly half of the year-round inhabitants of the small island town, and at least as many visiting vacationers and winter residents. Of course, in a town as small as Sunrise Key, the island visitors outnumbered the locals nearly six to one during the winter season.

The costumes Leila saw were as varied as their wearers. Many of them were charmingly homemade, but quite a few, like her own, had been rented.

Simon, looking dashing as Indiana Jones, was dancing with a mermaid. But not everyone was as easy to recognize. The light from the Japanese lanterns strung around the dance floor was dim at best, and many people had masks that covered their entire faces.

It was odd and slightly frightening—all of these people with hidden identities. With their faces carefully concealed behind masks, everyone had a certain bizarre freedom. For one night, they could actually become kings or clowns or veiled harem girls. Or Cinderella.

Leila spotted a second Batman dancing with a Catwoman, and she didn't have a clue as to who either of them were. At least three ninjas were scattered throughout the crowd, impossible to recognize beneath their masks.

"What are *you* dressed as?" Leila pulled her mask away from her face to look at Marsh more closely.

He was wearing khaki pants and a white shirt, the sleeves rolled up to his elbows.

"A harried, overworked small-town doctor." His sudden smile made him look boyishly handsome. "I just came from a house call. The youngest Knudsen boy got a piece of rust in his eye. Scratched his cornea. He'll be fine, but it hurts like the blazes. This has been a record-breaking week for the Knudsens. John Jr. knocked out his front tooth playing football—no helmet—and Melissa got seven stitches in her knee after trying to jump the curb in front of Millie's Market while wearing her Rollerblades."

Marsh looked tired. The lines around his eyes and mouth had deepened since Leila's last visit to the island, adding maturity to his face. Every year he became even more good looking. A lock of wavy brown hair had flopped forward into his eyes, but as usual he didn't seem to notice.

He never noticed when his hair was in his face. He simply looked through it. It drove Leila nuts.

"Have you made your New Year's resolutions?" Marsh asked.

"Funny you should ask," Leila muttered. In the past she hadn't had time for such things, but this year was different. Maybe it was because she'd just turned thirty. Maybe it was the impending second anniversary of her father's fatal heart attack. Or maybe it was Elliot's talk of marriage, but this year she'd spent the past few weeks looking back at her accomplishments and taking stock of where she was in life. Whatever the cause, never before had Leila felt so uncertain.

Careerwise, she couldn't have been happier. She had a thriving, successful private practice as an independent accountant in New York City. In a financial, business sense, she was precisely where she wanted to be. It was the other parts of her life—home, relationships, family— that were lacking. It was her personal life outside of the office that rated a big fat zero.

Even Elliot barely made a bump on her happiness index. But having children—babies—would make a difference. Wouldn't it?

"This year I have only one resolution," Marsh said. "To regain control of my life." He smiled ruefully. "Lately things have gotten rather out of hand."

"I was sorry to hear about the fire," Leila said. When her plane had landed at the tiny island airstrip, Simon had filled her in on all the local gossip. Leila's best friend, Frankie, had gotten her private investigator's license. Millionaire Preston Seaholm was back on the key, sans wife. Noah and Kim Kavanaugh were going to have a baby any minute now. The town committee had hired a new lifeguard for the town beach. And due to problems with the electric wiring, Marsh Devlin's big house on the point had recently burned to the ground.

Marsh smiled again, but this time it was tight and aloof, and kept his straight white teeth carefully hidden from view. "I'm sure you *were* sorry to hear that," he said. "Particularly since I'll be living here, in your brother's house, for God knows how long. Certainly for the two weeks you'll be visiting."

Marsh was over six feet tall, but Leila's high heels brought them directly eye to eye. "That's not what I meant," she said sharply.

"Sorry." He dropped his gaze, and with one hand finally, *finally* raked his hair back from his face. "Sorry, I'm . . . sorry. It's been miserable. I'm tired, and . . . sorry."

"How much did you lose in the fire?" Leila asked gently.

"Everything," he replied, glancing back up at her. Again, she could see a glimmer of fatigue in his eyes. "The place was gutted. Everything I owned went up in extremely literal smoke." He held out his arms. "I stand before you in borrowed clothes. I had one pair of jeans in my office, and a dozen dress shirts at the cleaners, but that—and the clothes I had on my back—was it."

"Oh, God, Marsh. I had no idea—"

"The worst of it was losing my pictures," he told her.

"You know, my collection of photographs? I had photos of Simon and you and me, back when Si and I were at university, and you were still just a little brat. I even had pictures from London. Pictures of my mother . . ."

He stared back at the colorful lights out in the yard. In the shadowy light, his face looked impossibly sad.

Leila was shocked.

In her experience, Marshall Devlin had only two emotional states. More often than not, he was detached and aloof. Occasionally he got angry and frustrated. And that was it. Leila had wondered if perhaps Marsh was incapable of experiencing all those other messy, complicated feelings. Sadness. Grief. Loneliness. Even the positive ones: happiness, excitement, joy, love. Especially love.

Looking at him now, seeing the pain and the loneliness etched on his face, Leila realized that he no doubt felt all of those things. He simply kept them carefully hidden. Neatly repressed.

What would it be like to chip away all of the chilly layers of Marsh's proper icy façade? Who would she find hiding there? The thought intrigued her. Obviously Marsh had been devastated by the fire. But before this moment, she hadn't believed him capable of being devastated by anything.

In all of the years she'd known him, Leila had never considered offering Marsh comfort. Before this very moment, she had never thought he'd ever need it. But he clearly did. And if he had been anyone else in the world, Leila would have put her arms around him and given him a hug. But this was Marsh Devlin standing in front of her.

So instead, Leila touched his arm. He felt solid and muscular. And warm. She could feel his body heat right through the sleeve of his shirt. He wasn't cold at all.

That was a silly thought. Of course he wouldn't feel cold to the touch. He was human, after all. His chilliness was in his demeanor. It wasn't a physical thing.

But as he glanced at her, surprised by her unexpected touch, there was a flash of warmth, of wonder on his face.

This was the first time she had ever touched Marshall Devlin, Leila thought almost inanely as she gazed into the green and gold flecks of his brown eyes. They'd spent the nineteen years since Marsh had first visited the island cautiously circling one another, battling with barbed words and acidic tongues, but never, ever touching. Wasn't that odd?

"I *am* sorry about the fire," she said. Looking down at her hand, she realized he'd covered it with his own. His fingers were bigger than hers and slightly roughened from outdoor work. They were very nice hands.

"Thanks, Leila," he said quietly. "I don't know how much Simon has told you, but things have been kind of tough lately."

He held her gaze steadily, and along with the pain and fatigue, she could see hope and warmth and promise. He was letting her see all that and more. He wasn't trying to hide any of it from her. It was another first.

Leila shook her head. "Simon hasn't told me anything." Her voice sounded breathless.

He looked away from her then, squinting at the ocean of partygoers moving on the dance floor. "Don't get me wrong," he said, glancing back at her. "I love it here on Sunrise Key. But I've been thinking—"

Before he could finish, a circus clown, a vampire, and a silent-film star came rushing across the lawn, leading a pack of about fifteen other partygoers toward the back deck of the house. They streamed around and between Marsh and Leila, and one of them, a harem girl, waved as she ran past.

"Hey!" she shouted over her shoulder. "Where's your fiancé? I thought you were bringing him along. What's his name?"

"Elliot," Leila called back. "And he's not my fiancé . . ." But the harem girl was gone. "Yet," she added lamely.

She glanced at Marsh again, but all of the depth and warmth he'd let her see was once more carefully concealed.

"You've been thinking . . . about what?" She knew that he wouldn't answer her, and silently cursed the sudden intrusion that had interrupted him.

"About Elliot," Marsh answered. "Look, I have to go up and change into my costume before Simon catches sight of me and arrests me for violating party rules."

Leila felt a stab of disappointment and frustration. He had been on the verge of opening up to her, on the brink of telling her something important and personal. But the mood had been broken. What had he been about to say? Why couldn't he talk to her that way—sincerely, and from the heart—all the time?

"Walk me back to the house, and tell me what detained this fellow of yours," Marsh continued. "Elliot. The man of your dreams, so to speak. Was it hell or high water?"

"Neither." Her gown made a *shush*ing sound on the ground as she walked. "It was work."

"Work. The worst of the four-lettered words. What is he, a doctor?" Marsh asked. "Was it some life-and-death emergency operation that only he could perform that's keeping him from your lovely side?"

Leila's frustration turned to sharp annoyance. "Not everyone is a critically important small-town doctor."

"Just curious." He ignored her insult. "New Year's Eve and Valentine's Day are the two most important holidays for lovers. It seems peculiar that he isn't here with you."

Leila and Elliot weren't lovers. Their relationship just hadn't progressed in that direction. At least not yet. And Leila was in no hurry to change that. But she wasn't about to correct Marsh and give him more ammunition to use against Elliot.

"One of his clients had an emergency," she said. "To be specific, a financial emergency. Elliot is a financial consultant."

"Splendid," Marsh said, far too enthusiastically. "It's truly comforting to know you're considering spending the rest of your life with a man who believes that having bags of money is more important than silly old love. Of course that works out rather nicely since you're not exactly in love with him, either."

Leila shook her head in exasperation. "Simon told

you about Elliot's proposal, didn't he? God, I don't know why I'm surprised. He tells you everything. There's no such thing as a secret on Sunrise Key, is there?"

"Ah, the great lack-of-privacy issue again. But this hasn't anything to do with that. When Si told me you were bringing this Elliot fellow with you, naturally, I asked some questions."

Leila shot him a look. "You don't honestly expect me to believe that there's a single person at this party who *hasn't* heard I was bringing a man to the island with me?"

"Of course not." Marsh held open the door to the house. "In a town this size, news of weddings and babies travels far and fast. Of course, everyone who's heard about Elliot assumes you're in love with the man. Only those privileged few of us know the real truth. I must say, marrying a man for his money . . . Somehow, I expected more from you, Leila."

"I'm not marrying Elliot for his money. If I marry him and that's a great big 'if'—it's because—" She broke off, suddenly unwilling to tell him her real reasons for considering marriage with Elliot. She couldn't bear to hear him mock her fears of spending her life alone, to have him ridicule her desires for children, for a family.

"My God." Marsh somehow managed to read her mind. "Something has unleashed the traditional female in you. It's time to have kids, so you latched on to the first idiot who came along!"

"Elliot's *not* an idiot," Leila said defensively. "It's true that I'm not exactly in love with him, but he's a good man, and I like him. If you don't like that, that's tough luck. But then again, why should I care? You've never liked anything I've ever done."

"Don't be ridiculous." Marsh's cool control was starting to slip. "Just because I was disappointed when you moved to New York City after college instead of back to the key—"

"Hah." Leila all but smacked him with her mask. "Disappointed because I wouldn't be around to torment and control. 'There goes Simon's little sister,' " she said in a mock English accent. " 'Let's see if we can get her *really* mad.' "

"What a load of rubbish," he muttered.

"It's *true*. And while you're at it, fix your stupid hair!"

"*My what?*" Marsh looked surprised. Was it possible he didn't notice that he was peering at her through an infuriatingly unkempt lock of hair?

"Leila's been home less than five hours, and you guys are *already* fighting?" a voice interrupted them. Simon, the mermaid clinging to his arm, stood in the doorway.

"Your hair is in your eyes," Leila told Marsh with exaggerated enunciation. "Most *normal* people would find that annoying and do something about it. Like *fix* it."

"I happen to like my hair just the way it is, thanks," Marsh said icily.

"You're arguing about Dev's *hair?*" Simon's voice dripped with amazement and disbelief.

"No, we're arguing because Leila's going to marry Elliot Something—I don't even know his last name—"

"Tillis," Leila supplied tightly.

"Right. Leila's only going to marry Elliot bloody Tillis because of some biological imperative to knit diamond-studded booties." Marsh pushed his hair out of his face. "Better now?" he said to Leila with overly done sweetness. But he didn't give her a chance to answer before turning back to Simon. "That's what this Elliot thing's about. She's afraid time's running out and she wants to have a baby. She doesn't even bloody well love this guy. Isn't that the stupidest bloody thing you've ever heard?"

"Maybe we can talk about this later," Simon said mildly. "After the party."

Marsh looked at Leila. "You know, you don't need to marry a man who doesn't love you simply to have a baby. Any man in the world can give you that. Axel Bayard could give you a baby. Old Martin Hampton could give you a baby. *I* could give you a baby."

Marsh's eyes were lit with the heat of anger as he glared at her. Anger, and a hint of something else. For an instant, his gaze raked her body, as if he were mentally undressing her. For an instant, her stomach felt as if she were riding a roller coaster. Gravity disappeared, and her insides flip-flopped.

Simon and the mermaid were watching her, waiting for her response to Marsh's loaded comment. What would Marsh do, Leila wondered wildly, if she said, *All right, I'll take you up on that.*

No doubt, knowing Marsh, he'd insist on going straight upstairs and "getting on with it, then." And, while she had to admit that the prospect of making love to her lifelong nemesis was extremely intriguing, where would she be in the long term?

Alone with a baby.

So, instead, Leila snorted. "Thanks, but I'd rather have Elliot's baby. I want to be married first. Being a single parent doesn't appeal to me."

"As if old Elliot's ever going to be around to change the kid's didee," Marsh said hotly.

"So what?" Leila crossed her arms. It was true that marriage to Elliot *would* mean spending quite a bit of time without him. But since Marsh was raising the point, Leila was forced to defend herself. "That doesn't mean I'll be alone. I'll be with the sweet Mary Poppins–type nanny that I can hire with Elliot's bags of money."

"Back to the money, are we?" Marsh said.

"Hey, are you guys going to fight the entire two weeks that Leila's here?" Simon asked.

"Yes," hissed Leila, turning on her glittering plastic heel and pushing her way out the door.

"Probably," Marsh said, stomping up the stairs.

TWO

Frankie Paresky, dressed as Cleopatra, was leaning against the bar that had been set up in the yard. With her shoulder-length dark hair and dark eyes, Leila's best friend on Sunrise Key looked spookily realistic, as if she'd stepped out of a stone tablet of hieroglyphics, or traveled forward in time.

"Welcome back," she shouted to Leila over the loud music, with a smile that quickly faded. "Uh-oh, what's wrong?"

"My brother's choice of friends, that's what." Leila stole a glass of wine from a nearby tray and took a long sip. "And these stupid plastic shoes are killing my feet."

"Are you and Marsh Devlin fighting again?" Frankie asked. "Of course you are. Dumb question. You two are in this year's revised copy of the dictionary under the word *argumentative*. You've been fighting ever since that very first vacation Marsh took down here with his dad."

"He is such an infuriating snob," Leila seethed.

"I don't know," Frankie said mildly in her gentle southern accent. "He's been real polite to me whenever I talk to him. But he's got that upper-class British thing happening, you know, as if his collar's too tight around his neck. Still, that doesn't make him a snob. He's just all backed up. I seriously doubt he acts that way intentionally."

"Yeah, well, what he does do intentionally is push my buttons," Leila said. "The man *loves* to torment me."

"I always thought he had some kind of thing for you. I swear I've seen him looking at you like he wants to gobble you up."

"Chew me up and spit me out is more like it." Still, an unbidden picture of Marsh's face as he told her *he* could give her a baby leaped into her mind.

Frankie smiled. "How are you?" she said, looking closely at Leila. "You look great. A little pale, but a few days on the beach'll take care of that. So where's this Yankee friend of yours?"

"Don't ask," Leila said.

"All right, I won't." Frankie changed the subject. "How's your mom? Simon told me she spent Christmas with you in New York."

"She's doing all right. It's hard for her to be here on the key now that Dad's gone, especially at this time of year. She's visiting relatives out west for a few weeks, then she's going on a cruise with my aunt Carol. She won't be back on Sunrise Key until February."

"She's smart," Frankie said. "Why stay here and get depressed?"

"Exactly."

"Hey, did you hear I got my private investigator's license?"

"Yeah. Congratulations. Simon told me the news. But . . ."

"There's not a lot of cases to solve here on Sunrise Key," Frankie finished for her. "I know, a place like this isn't exactly rampant with crime. But last week, Liam Halliday's office hired me as a consultant." She laughed, her dark brown eyes sparkling. "I picked through the school dumpster, looking for the Tennison girl's orthodontic retainer. Found it, too. A few more solid cases like that, and I'll be ready to write my memoirs."

"Liam Halliday." Leila took a handful of celery sticks from a platter on the bar, and shifted her weight to her right foot, the one that hurt the least. "The name rings a bell, but I can't place him."

"He's the sheriff," Frankie said. "Tall, broad shoulders, dark hair, brown eyes . . . ?"

Leila shook her head.

"Cowboy hat, Texas drawl, parties too hard . . . ?" Frankie continued.

Leila shrugged. "Maybe I've never met him. Or maybe I did and I just don't remember."

"If you'd met him, you'd remember him," Frankie said dryly. "He's cute as hell, a real good-time, good ol' boy. He's asked me out a few times, but I found excuses and turned him down. Going down to the Rustler's Hideout and slamming back a six-pack or two isn't my idea of a fun night out. I'm looking for a man who likes to spend a quiet evening at home, watching foreign films—and I'm not talking about Japanese monster movies."

"Good luck. Are you seeing anyone at all these days?" Leila asked.

Frankie shook her head and her big earrings jingled. "Nope."

"You're not still carrying a torch for Noah Kavanaugh, are you?"

"Too bad for me, if I were." Frankie rolled her eyes. "You know, he and Kim are having a baby. She's already a week past the due date."

"I heard that, too," Leila said. "And let's see, what else? Preston Seaholm is back in town."

"I saw his Rolls out front. I think he's here, somewhere, tonight." Frankie looked around at the crowd.

". . . without his wife," Leila said. "What's the scoop on *that?*"

"Apparently the new Mrs. Seaholm didn't marry Pres merely for his money. Turns out she was using him as a stepping-stone. He knows a bunch of movie producers based in Orlando, and one of 'em liked Mrs. S. enough to screen-test her and she landed a supporting role in a movie. Pres wasn't keen on spending eight months in Orlando, so he moved back here. Word has it, the divorce papers arrived in the mail less than a week after he was back. One thing's certain—you can bet Pres is thanking God and his attorneys for that prenup he had her sign."

"So he's single now." Leila traded her empty glass for a full one, wishing the wine would heal the blisters that were starting to form on her feet. Plastic shoes were the pits. Did Cinderella have this much pain from her glass slippers? Probably. Leila bet those fairy tales were written by a man. "Why don't you go out with him?"

Frankie laughed. "Oh, I am exactly Preston Seaholm's type . . . not! Good grief, Lei, the man's a billionaire, and I don't even have a hundred bucks in my checking account."

"So?"

"So, get real. He collects real estate for a living," Frankie said. "*I* dig through dumpsters."

"Simon told me there's another new guy in town. A lifeguard or something?"

"Hayden Young," Frankie told her. "Oh, baby. He can save my life *any*time. He's got the three essential *B*s."

"Which are . . . ?"

"Blond hair, blue eyes, and big biceps. Not to mention his various other muscles."

"Gee, and I thought one of those *B*s would stand for *brain*," Leila said wryly.

"Believe it or not, I think he's got one of them, too. He's working on getting a Ph.D. in got this—philosophy. He took this lifeguard job as a way to earn money while he sits around and thinks about his dissertation."

"He sounds perfect. Maybe he even watches foreign movies. Ask him out."

"I'd have to take a number and stand in line," Frankie said. "Every woman over the age of fourteen and under the age of one hundred is going to the beach and batting her eyelashes at the guy."

"Bummer."

"Yeah," Frankie agreed.

"Speaking of bummers, my feet are killing me."

"So take the shoes off. Be an authentic Cinderella, and drop one somewhere. It's almost midnight anyway. I don't know about you, but I want to grab a lounge chair so I can see Simon's fireworks without straining my neck."

"I'll catch up with you in a sec." Leila leaned down and pulled off her shoes. Oh, Lord, that was much better. She straightened up, then jumped back, alarmed. One of the ninjas was standing directly in front of her.

He was dressed all in black. Black sweat pants, black shirt, black sash around his waist, black shoes, and a black mask that covered his hair and all of his face, except for his mouth and chin. His eyes glittered colorlessly from two holes cut into the mask.

He wasn't really a ninja, Leila had to remind herself. He was only dressed like one. Still, he looked awfully mysterious.

Without warning, the lights dimmed even further, and the music kicked up in volume.

"Three minutes till countdown!" Simon's voice boomed over the p.a. system. "Three minutes left in the old year!"

"Dance with me," the ninja said. She couldn't hear him over the music, she could only read his lips.

She shook her head. Who was he? She couldn't identify him with that costume on. But he wouldn't take no for an answer. He took her hand and led her to the crowded dance floor.

The song was an old, slow, romantic tune, something

about night and day, day and night. The ninja pulled Leila close, holding him against her with a familiarity that was baffling. Who the heck *was* he?

His arms were solid—his whole body was solid and strong. She didn't know any men on Sunrise Key with a body like this. Except maybe Simon. But this sure wasn't her brother.

"Do I know you?" she whispered into the place under his mask where his ear should have been.

But he didn't answer her. He only held her closer, tightening his arm around her waist until she was fully pressed against him, from her knees all the way up to her chest. The dance floor was so full, it was impossible to do more than rock back and forth. Still, he moved gracefully.

And he smelled good. Fresh and clean, as if he'd just stepped out of a shower. It was that more than anything else that made Leila give in to the moment and rest her head on the man's shoulder. She felt him sigh, felt him touch the side of her face with gentle fingers, and she closed her eyes.

When was the last time she'd been held like this?

Not since she'd been dating Elliot, that much was for sure.

"Fifteen seconds to the new year!" Simon shouted, and Leila lifted her head as the crowd around them joined in with the countdown.

"Ten, nine, eight, seven . . ."

The ninja was watching her, and she stared back into his eyes, trying to guess their color in the dimness.

Hot. Whatever color they were, they were hot. He

wanted her—as if she didn't already know that from the intimate position of their bodies.

"Four, three, two, one! Happy New Year!" "Auld Lang Syne" blared from the loudspeakers.

"Happy New Year," the ninja soundlessly said to Leila.

And then he kissed her.

It started out as little more than a sweet brushing of his lips against hers.

Leila wasn't quite sure what happened, whether she was jostled by someone in the crowd, whether she lost her balance, or whether the ninja decided that one small taste was simply not enough and pulled her closer to him.

But suddenly, somehow, he was holding her even tighter, and her mouth had opened under his and he was *really* kissing her. It was a kiss of possession, a kiss of fire and flame, and Leila felt seared right to her heart. He tasted like champagne, seductively sweet, with one fantastically dangerous kick.

But just as suddenly as he'd begun, he pulled away.

Off balance, Leila wobbled, unsteady on her feet despite the fact that she'd taken off her high heels. She could see pure shock in the ninja's eyes, shock she knew was mirrored in her own face as he reached for her, to steady her. That had been one *hell* of an amazing kiss.

Above them, the sky exploded into color, and they both looked up to see fireworks streaming down like giant, glittering sparklers.

The ninja smiled. And then he kissed her again.

This time he didn't stop. He drank her in, inhaled her, devoured her in a long, slow, deep kiss as the music swirled around them, as the fireworks whistled and pounded and erupted overhead.

And, just as hungrily, Leila kissed him back. Her arms went around his neck, and her fingers explored the softness of his hair at the base of his hood.

Around them, people were laughing and dancing and blowing on noisemakers, but Leila shut them all out. Nothing mattered, nothing existed but this man, this . . . stranger, who was kissing her with all of the emotion, all of the heart and soul and passion of a long-lost lover.

"Auld Lang Syne" drew to a tremulous close, and without the music blaring, between bursts of fireworks, Leila slowly became aware that they were beeping. No, not them. The ninja.

She pulled back and he reached for her again, unwilling to let her go.

"You're beeping," she said.

He looked down in what might have been surprise—Leila didn't know—and sure enough, he was wearing a beeper attached to the waistband of his pants.

He opened his mouth to speak, and another song came on, obscuring his words. But he made a gesture with his hands that mimed a telephone, and Leila nodded.

"I'll be right back," he mouthed, rather than try to shout over the loud music. "Don't go anywhere."

Leila tried to protest. She opened her own mouth to

ask him to take off his mask, but he'd already been swallowed up by the crowd.

He didn't leave a shoe behind.

"You're always trying to convince me that along with being six years older than I am, you're also six years wiser." Leila and her brother sat on the deck overlooking the ocean, watching the sunrise.

As always, Simon was there for her. He was her brother, but he was also her friend—he had been for as long as Leila could remember. He'd never talked down to her. He'd always treated her as if she were a peer. Which, now that they were both in their thirties, she was.

But her friendship with her brother hadn't always been perfect. Back when Leila was younger, Marsh's visits to the island had brought discord to the otherwise harmonious relationship between the Hunt siblings. As a child, Leila had been jealous of Marsh and Simon's friendship. Jealous and a little awed. The two boys had as strong a bond as Leila and her best friend, Frankie, yet Marsh only lived on Sunrise Key during his vacations.

On the other side of the house, several of the more stalwart partygoers were still dancing. The music sounded ghostly as it was carried across the lawn and around the house by the wind.

Leila fingered the gossamer fabric of her Cinderella gown. "So tell me, oh wise one." She looked up to find Simon watching her over the rim of his coffee cup.

"What the heck is wrong with me, that I would kiss a total stranger as if the world were coming to an end?"

Simon sat forward, pushing the brim of his hat back to see her better in the predawn light. "You mean, like, tongues?"

"Totally. This man now knows the inside of my mouth better than my dentist."

Simon laughed. "Wow. How unlike you."

"No kidding," Leila said morosely. "I've kissed exactly five men in my entire life. And before I kissed them, I knew their complete background and history. I knew how many parking tickets they'd ever received and whether or not they paid them on time. I knew the names of their kindergarten teachers. I knew their SAT scores and their GMATs. I knew their favorite flavor of ice cream and whether they liked sugar cones or those other icky waffle ones. It was ludicrous. I kissed this guy and actually saw fireworks."

"There *were* fireworks," Simon pointed out.

"It's crazy." Leila ignored him. "I lost my balance. He swept me off my feet."

"Maybe you had too much champagne," Simon suggested.

"Two dinky glasses? That can't be it."

"Who is he?" Simon asked, taking a sip of coffee.

"That's my point here, Si. I honestly don't know. His beeper went off, and he went dashing out of here. He said don't go anywhere. He said he'd be right back. But he vanished. I spent the rest of the night looking for him." Leila stared out at the water, watching it reflect the glow of light in the east. "God, am I stupid, or what?"

"You don't even have a clue?"

Leila exhaled in exasperation. "All I know is that he's taller than I am. How much taller I can't tell you. He's male, he's strong, he wears a beeper, and he looks good in black. How many men did you invite to this party? A hundred? That description should fit, oh, ninety-five of 'em."

"What kind of costume was he wearing?" Simon asked. "Maybe I know who he was."

"Ninja," Leila said. "He was a ninja."

"Hmmm." Simon took another pensive sip of coffee. "That's a tough one. I don't think I talked to a single ninja all night. I saw at least four of them, but I wasn't sure who they were. You know, the mask and everything."

"My point exactly."

"So what does this mean?" Simon stretched his long legs and rested his cowboy-booted feet on the deck railing. "You're frenching it with some other guy while old what's-his-name, the guy who wants to marry you, isn't around?"

"Ugh, you make it sound so tawdry," Leila moaned.

"It *wasn't* tawdry?" he asked.

"No! It was . . ."

"What?"

"Magic." Leila closed her eyes and let her head fall back. "Oh no, did I just say that?"

"I heard you say magic." Simon chuckled. "Thank God."

Leila's eyes shot open. "Thank *God?!* Whose side are you on? I'm losing my mind and you're giving prayers of thanks?"

"It's just that I was afraid you were actually going to say yes to this Elliot bozo and never give yourself a chance to really fall in love."

Leila stared at her brother. His hair was blond, like hers, but wavy, not curly. His face was handsome, with refined features. His nose was perfectly sculpted with slightly flaring nostrils, his lips were graceful yet masculine, his chin strong without being mulishly stubborn. His eyes were a truer shade of blue than hers, surrounded by long, thick, dark eyelashes that seemed to be nature's way of laughing at all of the women who spent a fortune on mascara.

Her brother's face was elegant, Leila thought sourly. Didn't it figure.

"I think," Simon continued, "that maybe you're in love with this ninja, whoever he is."

Leila laughed, a quick, loud burst of disbelieving air. "You think I'm in *love* with someone that I not only have never met, but that I've never actually laid eyes on?"

"Stranger things have happened." Simon shrugged. "They say there's a perfect match for everyone. Maybe this guy's perfect for you, and deep down, you recognized that."

Leila rolled her eyes. "I'd rather go with the too-much-champagne theory."

Footsteps on the stairs leading up to the deck made Leila sit up. Maybe it was the ninja. Maybe he was coming back.

But it was only two of Simon's friends, coming to say good night before they left.

Simon didn't stand up as he shook the couple's hands, and as Leila excused herself, she felt his eyes on her. She knew he'd picked up on the fact that she was still waiting—like a fool—for that damned ninja to come back.

Leila went into the house, gathering up a trayful of champagne glasses and little plates as she headed toward the kitchen. Simon was a firm believer in recycling, and he never used paper or plastic if he could help it. He'd rented thick, unbreakable glasses and plates from a caterer up in Venice. And he'd hired a local team of cleaners—most of whom had also attended the party—to come over that afternoon and get everything washed and picked up. Still, it couldn't hurt to help.

And as long as she was helping with the cleaning, she didn't have to think.

She didn't have to think about Elliot's plane landing on the tiny island in a matter of hours. She didn't have to think about her conversation with Simon. And mostly, she didn't have to think about the mysterious man who had kissed her and disappeared.

Where had he gone? Why hadn't he come back?

How was it possible that she'd fallen in love *and* had her heart broken all in the span of a few short hours?

Oh, no way, she told herself firmly. The things Simon had been saying to her were making her confused, that's all. Tonight's little adventure had nothing to do with love. She was simply overtired, that was it.

Still, she couldn't deny that those kisses were incomparable to anything she'd ever experienced before.

"Hey, Cinderella."

Leila looked up to see Marsh Devlin standing in the kitchen door.

"I was sure you'd have turned into a pumpkin long before this," he said, leaning against the doorframe. He was wearing his bathing suit and a T-shirt, with a towel draped over one shoulder. His hair was wet, and, naturally, it flopped down into his eyes. With an apologetic smile, Marsh raked his hair back, out of his face. "If I'd've known you were awake, I'd've asked you to join me for a swim."

"What are you doing up?" Leila asked, drying her hands on a towel. "I thought you'd gone to bed hours ago."

Marsh frowned slightly. "Didn't Simon tell you?"

"Tell me what?"

"About the baby."

Leila stared at Marsh blankly.

"Kim Kavanaugh went into hard labor shortly before midnight. I had to get over to the clinic quickly. I asked Simon to tell you."

Leila shook her head. "He never mentioned it. His mermaid friend got all jealous when he danced with Alice in Wonderland, so he was a little distracted. Was it a girl or a boy?"

Now it was Marsh's turn to blink at her. But he caught on quickly enough.

"Girl. Born about half three this morning. Mother and daughter were doing fine, so I came back a little while ago to get some rest." He smiled. "I should've known you'd still be up."

Marsh had been out all night, delivering a baby. That explained his oddness, his nervousness, why he was looking at her so strangely.

Leila sank down into one of the kitchen chairs. Boy, she was tired. How could Marsh stay out all night delivering a baby and look so refreshed, so *good?* And as long as she was lamenting foolishly, why did he have to be so damned handsome? "Congratulations."

"Thanks. But truth be told, Kim did most of the hard work. Good thing she was there to calm Noah and me down."

Leila snorted, resting her chin in her hand. "You're the King of Calm. I'm sure you were fine."

Marsh shook his head. "This was my fourteenth baby. I have delivered thirteen others. But each one is as if it's the first, Leila. I hold that brand new baby in my hands, and it's . . . magic. It's fantastic. It's impossibly miraculous."

He came into the kitchen, took the teapot off the stove, and filled it with water. "Of course, right now everything seems rather impossibly miraculous," he continued, tossing another smile in her direction as he lit the burner of the gas stove.

Leila stared at him. He was positively humming with happiness. She'd never seen him like this before. It made him seem charmingly sweet—and amazingly attractive. She had to pull her eyes away from the firm muscles of his back that were stretching the thin cotton of his T-shirt. That was funny. She'd always thought of him as skinny—attractive, but skinny. Where had all those muscles come from? She tried to remember the last time she'd seen him in a T-shirt, but she couldn't.

God, what was wrong with her tonight? First she kissed a total stranger and now she was openly ogling Marsh.

"I *am* sorry that I had to run out of the party," he said.

"Simon outdid himself this time." Leila rested her head on the table. "It was a terrific party. It's too bad you missed it."

Marsh rummaged through the cupboards, searching for the tea tin. "I hope it didn't get *too* much better after I left." He glanced at her over his shoulder.

If he only knew. . . .

"Can I interest you in a cup of tea?" He took two mugs out of the cabinet, holding one in each hand as he turned to face her.

He wanted desperately to talk, Leila knew that much from the strange light in his brown eyes. But he wanted to talk about new babies and miracles, and all she could think about was who the heck had kissed her at midnight, and what all these feelings burbling around inside of her meant. And why on *earth* did the mystery man's failure to return make her ache so badly?

"I'm sorry," she said. "I'm not up for it right now."

"But Leila—"

"Marsh, Elliot's going to be here by dinnertime, and I suddenly feel as if my entire world's turned upside down." Yes, that was truly what it felt like. It felt as if someone had come into her life and taken all of her neat and tidy shelves and cabinets and pushed them over, into a big, disorganized pile. She wanted to get it all back into at least some semblance of order before Elliot showed up. But something told her it wasn't going to be that easy.

On the stove, the kettle began to whistle. Marsh turned off the heat.

"Elliot. Of course. Right. I'd forgotten about him. Silly of me, really. Have you decided how you're going to tell him—I mean, I'll help you, you know. If you want . . ."

Leila stared at Marshall. "Tell him?"

"About what happened at the party." His wet hair fell forward into his face, and he swiped at it with his towel. "I mean, it *does* seem rather significant and—"

"Oh, this is *perfect!*" Leila exploded. "I should've known Simon couldn't keep a secret. He told you everything, didn't he? About the fireworks and . . . everything?"

"Simon?" Marsh frowned. "What did he—"

"This is just great." Leila stood up so suddenly that the chair she'd been sitting in fell backward with a crash. How could Simon have done this to her? How could he have told Marsh Devlin—of all people—about that amazing, fabulous, devastating kiss? How *could* he? But of course, Simon told Marsh, Leila realized. Simon told Marsh everything. Private matters weren't private for long on Sunrise Key. Leila was a fool for thinking otherwise.

But now Marsh knew her deepest, darkest, most terrible secret. How wretchedly awful. How totally, mind-numbingly humiliating. "I'm never going to hear the end of this, am I?"

"Leila, what are you—"

"Damn you, and damn Simon and . . . and . . . damn *everything!*"

Leila hiked up the skirt of her ball gown and ran from the room, leaving Marsh staring after her.

What in bloody hell was going on?

His tea long since forgotten, Marsh went in search of the man he suspected held the answers to all of his questions.

Simon.

THREE

"And Leila honestly doesn't know who kissed her?" Marsh asked.

Simon looked closely at his friend, and Marsh smiled wryly, knowing without a doubt that he'd just given himself away.

"My God, it was *you*," Simon said.

Marsh sat down wearily in the deck chair next to Simon's and stared out at the ocean. "It was me," he admitted.

"But, Dev, that's great."

"*Was* great," Marsh corrected him. "Past tense. Right now it's not so great after all." All of his elation, all of the euphoria that had come from having Leila— lovely, brilliant, sparkling, gorgeous Leila—in his arms had long since vanished. True, he'd kissed her at midnight, but she hadn't kissed him. At least, not knowingly. "What the hell was she doing anyway, kissing a total bloody stranger like that?"

Simon poured himself another cup of coffee from the thermos next to him on the table. "Don't be so British. The important thing here is that Leila's not going to marry that bozo, Elliot."

"Oh, and what?" Marsh didn't hide his skepticism. "I suppose you think now she's going to marry *me*."

Simon took a long sip of his coffee. "Is that what you want?"

Marsh looked into his friend's clear blue eyes and found not a trace of recrimination, prejudgment, or blame. There was only trust . . . and friendship. Years and years of true friendship.

The truth was, Marsh wanted—desperately—to make love to Leila. He wanted to love her in the very physical sense of the word. But . . . marriage? The thought was extremely appealing. Leila—permanently his. But it was also terrifying.

"I don't know," he said finally. "All I know is, I'm in love with your sister, Simon. I think I have been for years. It's just . . ."

Even with Simon, who knew him better than anyone on earth, it was so hard to open up. And what was he supposed to say? That he was scared to death? Scared that Leila wouldn't love him . . . and scared to hell that she would? Scared she'd actually marry him . . . and then turn around and leave him someday, the way his father and mother had left each other?

"I'm terrified," Marsh admitted.

Simon handed Marsh the coffee mug. "I know. I would be, too."

Marsh stared down into the steaming brown liquid.

"Shouldn't you be offering me something a bit stronger?"

Simon grinned. "Trust me. It's in there."

Marsh took a sip. The coffee itself wasn't that hot, but whatever it was that Simon had added to the brew burned all the way down to his stomach. He handed the mug back and they sat for a few moments in silence.

"Leila's angry at you," Marsh said. "She thinks you let slip her secret."

"Well, that'll get taken care of soon enough. As soon as she realizes it was you, as soon as you tell her—"

"No." Marsh sat forward. "She can't be told. I can't tell her—"

"Oh, come on, Dev—"

"No, Simon, really." Good Lord, if Leila found out that he was the one who kissed her last night, it would be an absolute disaster. "What am I supposed to do? Walk up to her and say, 'Oh, by the way, it was I, the one man in the universe you're most likely to argue with, the man you don't even like, who kissed you so soundly at midnight'? Is that what I'm supposed to say?"

"I guess you've got a point."

"I don't want her to feel as if I've made a fool of her, or to hate me," Marsh said quietly. "In fact, I want quite the opposite."

"And you think by *not* telling her the truth, you have a better shot at that?"

Marsh sighed and rubbed his hands across his face. "You make it sound so bloody dishonest."

"Just tell me what you want me to do," Simon said.

"Don't tell her it was me," Marshall answered. "Please? I'll tell her. I promise. Just not yet."

Simon nodded. "You better not blow this. I don't want some bozo for a brother-in-law." He laughed. "At least not any bozo besides you."

"That's *Doctor* Bozo, to you."

Simon grinned. "Happy New Year, by the way."

"Right. It's new, anyway."

Leila sipped a glass of soda and watched as Simon prepared one of his stir-fried vegetables-and-tofu concoctions for dinner. He was actually a better-than-decent cook, and the tofu stuff he made always tasted very good, but Leila hated seeing it in its precooked phase—a white brick of soy protein, all pale and quivering on the cutting board.

"What time is Elliot's flight coming in?" Simon asked as he cut the tofu into neat little bite-sized squares.

Leila glanced at her watch. "Eight o'clock. Two hours."

Simon looked up at her. "I'm surprised you didn't call him and beg off. You know, tell him you don't want him to come. Politely, of course."

Leila pulled her legs up to sit cross-legged on the kitchen chair. "Actually, I'm looking forward to seeing him."

Simon stopped cutting and stared at her. "You are?"

"I lost it last night," she admitted. "Number one, I kissed a total stranger, and number two, those kisses apparently meant nothing to this stranger, because he left the party without a single look back." She took a deep breath. "He obviously doesn't care about a few silly little kisses, and neither do I."

Simon grinned. "Is that why you carried the portable phone down to the beach this afternoon? Because you didn't care whether or not this mystery guy was going to call you?"

"I thought *Elliot* was going to call," Leila said with great dignity. It figured that Simon would notice that she had carried the phone around all day.

Seeing Elliot would do her good, she tried to tell herself. He was so down to earth, so . . . well, unromantic. But that was okay. She knew his limitations. She wouldn't have to worry about becoming disappointed with him twenty years down the road.

Because he was already so disappointing.

Leila looked up at her brother as he chopped broccoli into small pieces. That last thought, although it sounded quite a bit like something Simon might say, had come from some dark, disenchanted corner of her very own mind.

The honest truth was, Leila didn't want to see Elliot. In fact, she was dreading his arrival. She'd spent the entire afternoon frustrated and restless, and the last thing she wanted right now was to listen to Elliot drone on and on about his latest business dealings.

What she wanted to do was find that man who'd kissed her. And then what? Well, she'd probably start by kissing him again.

Out in the hallway, the front door squeaked open

and then shut. "Identify yourself," Simon called cheerfully.

"It's only me." Marsh carried his briefcase and doctor's bag into the kitchen, his jacket over his arm. "Are you expecting someone else?" He glanced at Leila. "You got some sun today."

"You look awful," she said.

Marsh was positively drooping with exhaustion and heat. His hair was damp, curling slightly at the ends. He'd taken off his tie and was unbuttoning the top buttons of his shirt as he sank down into a chair on the other side of the kitchen table. "I give you a compliment, and you tell me I look awful?"

Leila made a face at him, then stood to pour him a glass of iced tea. "Since when is 'You got some sun today' considered a compliment?"

Marsh frowned. "Is that what I said?" he mused. "Sorry." He took the glass from Leila, and their fingers accidentally brushed. "Thanks." He set the glass down in front of him. "I meant to say you look lovely this evening. More so, even, than you usually do."

He smiled, and Leila knew he was smiling at the astonishment he could see in her eyes. Since when did Marsh give her such lavish compliments?

Simon added a variety of spices and sauces to the already sizzling stir fry. "Are you here for good, or are you going back out again?"

Marsh took a long sip of his iced tea. "I've got one more trip over to the Kavanaugh's, to check on the new baby, but not till later tonight." He took a deep breath and let it out quickly. "Good Lord, I can't get by on two hours of sleep any longer. Remind me to go to bed before dawn tonight."

"Why don't you take a nap?" Simon suggested.

"And miss what's-his-name's arrival? Definitely not."

"Elliot," Leila said. "He has a name, and it's Elliot."

Marsh gazed across the table at Leila, who was drawing circles in the condensation from her glass. She glanced up and met his eyes, and to his surprise, she blushed and looked away. Blushed? Since when did Leila get embarrassed around him? Angry, yes. Annoyed, most likely. But embarrassed? That was strange.

Lord, but she did look lovely tonight. Her wild array of golden curls were cut in a short cap around her face, creating a perfect frame for her eyes. And what eyes! They were a beautiful violet shade of blue Marsh had never seen before on a living, breathing human being. And those eyes could hold the warmth of the sun, dancing and sparkling with a happiness that was truly contagious. They also had the power to freeze him with one crystal, icy look. But filled with tears, laden with sadness, Leila's eyes could bring him to his knees.

Her smile was the same. Wide and infectious, her smile embraced everything and everyone around her, letting the entire world in on the joke. It seemed amazing to Marsh that lips so delicate and elegantly shaped could curl upward into such an unabashedly joyful smile.

Of course, he'd always imagined that kissing Leila's lips would be rather like kissing a fairy princess—exquisitely light and delicate. And kissing her had been exquisite, but in a different sort of way. It had been deep and rich and sensual and utterly, thoroughly soul shattering.

One kiss, and all of the secrets he'd been hiding from himself for so long had been exposed. He loved her. He was in love with this wonderful, gorgeous, *maddening* woman. Yes, he was in love, and he had been for years.

Two kisses and Marsh knew the true meaning of the word euphoria. Because she loved him, too. Leila *had* to love him, too. There was no way on God's green earth she could kiss him like that and not at least feel something for him.

But he had been wrong. She didn't love him. She didn't even like him. She hadn't known whom she was kissing.

Sitting there in Simon's kitchen, watching Leila, Marsh finally figured out what to do.

He had to court Leila. Slowly, carefully. He had to let her get to know him—*really* know him.

Marsh had to let down all of his defenses and let her truly see him. And he had to pray to God that she would like what she saw.

It was, quite possibly, going to be the hardest thing he'd ever done. Of course, this was Leila, not some stranger he'd just met. In some ways, that made the whole thing easier. But in others, it made it infinitely harder.

What if Marsh opened up to Leila and she rejected him? What if he told her something personal, something private, and she used it to tease him, to ridicule him? He might never recover.

Still, he had to try to show her that the fire that

sparked their frequent arguments and disagreements could be harnessed. True, their relationship tended to be volatile. They'd probably never stop quarreling entirely, they were both too sharp-tongued for that. But think how sweet making up could be. And just thinking about redirecting the heat and sparks that snapped between them—redirecting them into the bedroom—was dizzying.

Sooner or later, Marsh was going to have to reveal that he was the man who'd kissed Leila last night at midnight. Sooner rather than later, since she was only going to be on the key for the two short weeks of her vacation.

But two weeks were better than no weeks, and he was determined to use as much time as he had available to make Leila like him. And he *would* make her like him. Because she had to like him before she could fall in love with him.

He couldn't shake the feeling that his house burning down had been some sort of signal from a higher deity. It was the end of one part of his life and the beginning of another. A new beginning. Time to rise from the ashes and make a fresh start. Take a chance.

Across the room, the phone rang. Simon's stir-fry was sizzling and he was cooking with both hands, but he reached out and punched a button on the telephone that was attached to the wall. "Hello?" he called. "You're on the speaker phone. Keep it clean."

"Yes," said a male voice. "I'm looking for Leila Hunt?"

Leila leaned forward, a frown creasing her forehead. "Elliot?"

"Yes, it's me," he answered.

"This signal's awfully clean. Are you calling from the plane?" she asked.

There was a pause before he replied. "No, I'm sorry, I'm not, Leila."

Elliot *wasn't* on the plane? Marsh didn't let himself smile. At least, not outwardly. Inside, he was turning cartwheels.

"I'm sorry," Elliot's voice continued, "but I'm not going to make it down this weekend after all."

Leila stood up, her chair scraping across the kitchen floor. "Simon, I'm going to take this in the other room." She started out the door, then turned back. "Make sure you hang up when I pick up the extension."

"What, do you think we'd eavesdrop?"

"Yes. Don't." With a stern look that included Marsh, Leila swept out of the room.

As Marsh watched, Simon took three plates from the cabinet and spread them out on the kitchen counter.

"Hello?" Leila's voice came out of the telephone's speaker.

"Hey, kiddo. I'm really sorry about this—"

"Simon, hang it up!" Leila shouted from the other room.

Simon reached over and pushed a button. "Okay," he shouted back.

But Marsh could still hear Elliot's voice over the speaker. "Simon . . ." he said warningly.

"We can hear them," Simon said with a grin, "but they can't hear us. She'll never know."

"I stand to make seven figures on this deal alone." Elliot's voice was tinny over the speaker. "I just can't pass that up."

Marsh crossed the kitchen, gazing at the telephone as if that would shut it off. "Leila wanted privacy."

Simon shook his head. "Aw, you're no fun now that you're in love with her."

Marsh winced, looking quickly toward the other room. "Shh!"

"She can't hear us."

"We shouldn't be listening," Marsh insisted. "How do you turn this thing off?"

"How about next weekend?" Leila's voice asked. "Will you make it down here next weekend?"

"Say no." Marsh stared at the speakerphone, willing Elliot to answer with a negative. His desire to hang up the phone and give Leila privacy was forgotten. "You're far too busy. You can't possibly find time to visit."

There was a pause, then Elliot said, "I'm looking at my calendar, and I don't know . . ." He sighed. "Right now, I've got to say no, Leila. I'm way too busy. It's a bad time of year. But I'll tell you what. If you can get back to New York a few days early, I promise that we can have lunch."

"Of all the pompous, condescending, outrageous, *pompous*—"

"You already said that." Simon carefully balanced and carried all three of the plates toward the sliding doors that led to the back deck. "Hit the kill switch on the phone, will you? It's the button on the top left."

"I'll call you in a few days," Elliot's voice was saying as Marsh pushed the button and the speaker clicked off.

"He's dreadful." Marsh followed Simon onto the deck.

"He's not quite as bad as I imagined," Simon said, "but he's close."

"She's not going to marry him," Marsh said hotly. "I'm sorry. I simply won't allow it."

"You won't *allow* it?"

Marsh turned to see Leila standing in the doorway.

"What was that odd click I heard just as Elliot was saying good-bye?" she asked.

Simon shrugged. "Probably just the telephone line making noises. Interference."

"You are *such* a lousy liar," Leila said. "Why do you even bother?"

"Dinner's ready. Who wants wine?" Simon vanished into the kitchen.

Leila turned to face Marsh. "And *you*. You're not going to *allow* me to marry Elliot?"

"Lei, I gotta agree." Simon came back out onto the deck carrying three glasses, a bottle of white wine, and a bottle of soda. "Elliot's . . . well . . . he's . . ."

"He's an ass," Marsh said flatly.

Simon grinned, pouring a glass of wine for himself and Leila, and a glass of soda for Marsh. "Two extra days in sunny Florida in December . . . in exchange for lunch with Elliot. Is that supposed to be some kind of fair trade?"

"That click was just interference on the phone line, huh?" Leila crossed her arms. "You guys listened in on that whole conversation, didn't you?"

Marsh shifted his weight guiltily. They had. They'd eavesdropped, fulfilling all of Leila's dark expectations regarding her privacy—or lack of privacy—on Sunrise Key.

But Simon just sat down and started to eat his dinner. "This is getting cold. You guys should eat."

Marsh knew that he should tell Leila he was sorry. They'd violated her privacy, and that was wrong. But the words that came out of his mouth were not at all apologetic. "I have to warn you. If you insist on marrying Elliot, I intend to stand up and loudly proclaim my unhappiness when the reverend says, 'Speak now or forever hold your peace.' And for an encore, I will throw you over my shoulder and carry you out of there, kicking and screaming if need be."

"You wouldn't dare." Leila's voice dripped with disbelief. "You'd never create such a scene."

"Just try me," Marsh threatened.

"Fine, I won't send you an invitation." Leila crossed her arms.

"Oh, *that* will surely keep me away."

"Yo, guys?" Simon interjected. "Food's getting cold."

"What could Leila possibly have been thinking?" Marsh said. "I mean, did she actually sit down and think, 'Golly, I'd like to have some children. Let me see if I know any idiots I can join in a loveless marriage in order to conceive them."

Leila's eyes flashed with anger. "I happen to know that Elliot's IQ is a great deal higher than the average—"

"Leila, I have that copy of the party's guest list that you wanted," Simon interrupted.

Leila's mouth shut as absolutely as if Simon had pressed a button and turned her off. She stared at Simon, glancing once at Marsh, as if hoping he hadn't heard her brother's words.

"Guest list?" Marsh's anger and frustration instantly evaporated. Why would Leila want a list of guests for a party that had already happened?

"You might at least have waited until we were alone," Leila said to Simon through clenched teeth.

"Yeah, well, I figured both Marsh and I could help you," Simon replied.

"For the New Year's party?" Marsh asked, looking from Leila to Simon. "*That* guest list?"

"She wouldn't tell me why she wants it," Simon said. "But my guess is that she's going to try to track down this guy who kissed her." He grinned at Marsh "Remember, the guy I *told* you about?"

"Argh." Leila sank into her seat at the table and buried her face in her hands.

"Simon," Marsh began. The last thing he wanted was to embarrass Leila. But Simon held up his hand, stopping him.

"Look, Lei," Simon said. "It's too late to pretend that Marsh doesn't know what happened last night. I'm going to help you, right? He might as well help, too. If two heads are better than one, think of how terrific three will be."

"Terrific," Leila muttered.

"Do you really want to find this man?" Marsh asked, hardly daring to hope.

She looked up at him. "Yes," she admitted with a sigh. "Yes, I do. I know it sounds crazy but—"

"That's *great*," Marsh said. "It's not crazy, it's great."

"I need to find this ninja," Leila continued, "so that I can prove to myself he wasn't real. I didn't even know who he was. Whatever I felt from kissing him *had* to have been the result of too much champagne, or I don't know, lust, or the phase of the moon. It just wasn't real. I mean, I'm probably going to find him, and he'll turn out to be someone I absolutely hate, right?"

"So why bother going to all the trouble of tracking this bozo down?" Simon asked.

"Ninja," Marsh corrected him. "Not bozo."

Leila looked out into the starry darkness of the sky. She was quiet for several long moments. "Doubt," she finally said. "Just the barest, smallest sliver of doubt." She glanced back at Marsh and he saw there were actually tears in her eyes. "I just keep thinking, what if . . ."

"That's not doubt," Marsh told her. "That's hope. Hope that there really is one special person out there just waiting for you to find him."

Leila blinked back her tears. "God, I wish you were right."

"Are you so sure I'm not?"

❖━━━━━━━━━❖

"John McGrath?" Leila read from Simon's long, hand-scribbled list of names.

"Cross him off, too." Simon tipped his chair back and rested his bare feet on the highly polished antique dining room table. "I saw him with some kind of Roman toga thing on."

"Very original, old John is," Marsh commented.

"How about Paul Casella?" Leila asked.

"Didn't see him," Simon said.

"He brought a date," Marsh volunteered. "A young woman he's been seeing for the past few months, lives on the mainland. They came as Bonnie and Clyde."

"Oh, yeah," Simon added. "Big plastic submachine guns."

"That was Paul."

Leila crossed Paul's name off.

"Preston Seaholm?"

Simon and Marsh looked at each other blankly.

"Was he even at the party?" Marsh asked.

"Dunno," Simon responded. "*I* didn't see him."

"Frankie said she saw his car," Leila said.

"I guess that makes him a suspect," Simon said. "Seaholm's tall enough, right?"

Leila nodded. "But remember, I don't know exactly how tall the ninja was. I just had this sensation that he was taller than me."

"And that he was strong," Marsh reminded her. Simon coughed.

"And that he carries a beeper," Leila added. "Does Pres Seaholm have a beeper?"

"I don't know," Simon said. "But that wouldn't be too hard to find out."

Marsh looked over Leila's shoulder, quickly skimming through the list of names. His own name was up at the top of the page. Leila had apparently skipped him. He wasn't sure whether to feel insulted or relieved. "Who's next? Keith Banner? I don't remember seeing him at the party."

"Same here," Simon said. "And I know *he's* got a beeper."

"Nope." Leila crossed Keith's name off the list. "It's not Keith."

"Did you see him, then?" Marsh asked.

"Nope."

"How can you be so sure?" Simon asked.

Leila carefully laid her pen down on the table. "If you must know, I've had the dubious honor of being kissed by Keith Banner before. He's an octopus. My ninja was not."

"Octopus?" echoed Marsh, frowning slightly.

"Eight hands," Simon explained.

"Oh," Marsh said. "Right. Of course. Octopus."

"My ninja was a gentleman."

"*Your* ninja." Simon lifted his eyebrows as he glanced at Marsh.

"There were three other ninjas at the party," Leila pointed out. "I don't want to get mine confused with the others. Sean Green. How about Sean Green?"

She looked at Simon and he smiled happily back at her. He was actually enjoying himself, the wretch.

"Sean came as Dracula." Simon watched as Leila crossed that name off the list.

"The final name is—drum roll please!—Liam Halliday," Marsh announced. "The esteemed sheriff of Sunrise Key. I, for one, didn't see him last night."

"Neither did I," Simon said. "But isn't he way too tall?"

"He is rather tall," Marsh agreed.

"I'm going to include him among the suspects anyway," Leila decided, "because although I don't remember my ninja being extremely tall, I don't remember him *not* being extremely tall."

"So, how many does that give us?" Simon asked.

"Six." She counted them off on her fingers. "Hayden Young, Robert Earle, Alan Lanigan, Bruce Kimble, Preston Seaholm, and Liam Halliday. Except for Robert Earle, whom we know nothing about, they're all single, they all RSVP'd they'd be coming, and they all possibly carry a beeper."

"Are you sure you got everybody?" Simon asked.

Leila flipped through the pages, scanning the list of names.

Marsh. She'd missed Marsh.

Was it possible?

She glanced over her shoulder to find him watching her. One elegant eyebrow rose slightly as he evenly returned her gaze, and she turned away. No. No way. She just couldn't see Marsh kissing her the way that ninja had kissed her. Those kisses had been pure rocket fuel, relentlessly combustible and unrestrained. That was hardly Marsh's style. She could imagine Marsh kissing her carefully, sweetly, without managing to mess up her hair or even smear her lipstick.

"Now what?" Marsh asked. "Do you intend to line them all up and kiss them, then?"

Leila twisted her head to look up at him again. "Line them up, no. Kiss them, yes."

"You're kidding," Simon said flatly.

"How else am I going to prove to myself that what happened last night was just an aberration or a fluke?"

Simon exchanged another look with Marsh.

"What if it wasn't?" he asked.

"I don't know," Leila admitted. "I haven't really considered that possibility."

"You better," Simon said. "You better be ready for anything. What if this guy is Mr. Wonderful?"

"That's unlikely."

"Assuming he's Mr. Wonderful is reaching a bit," Marsh interjected. "I mean, 'Mr. Wonderful' is expecting too much, don't you think?"

"What if he is?" Simon persisted.

"First things first, all right?" Leila said. "And first I've got to narrow this list down. There were only four ninjas at the party. Only four of these six guys could be real suspects."

"What are you going to do?" Simon asked. He pulled his feet off the table and leaned forward, resting his chin in his hand as he studied his sister's face. "Call them up and ask what they wore to the party?"

Leila shook her head. "No. I'm going to hire Frankie. She's a private investigator."

Simon hooted with laughter. "Frankie? Get real, Lei. What did she do, get a fedora and a trenchcoat from the Private Eye Store? And now she thinks she's a real PI?"

"She got her license, Simon. You told me that yourself."

"I could get a piece of paper that says I'm president of the United States," Simon retorted. "That doesn't make it true."

"She *did* find Becca Tennison's retainer," Marsh pointed out.

"Sherlock Holmes is shaking in his shoes," Simon said.

"Everybody has to start somewhere." Leila stood up and stretched. "Do you remember how everyone scoffed when *you* decided to become an art and antiques dealer?"

"Yes. And I also remember that Francine Paresky scoffed particularly loudly. It's payback time."

"Speaking of payback time," Leila said, "you guys owe me an apology for eavesdropping on my conversation with Elliot."

"I *am* sorry," Marsh murmured.

"I'm not." Simon leaned back in his chair. "And I still think the guy's a jerk for standing you up this weekend. He said he was coming down here with you. He shouldn't have let business get in his way."

"The deal he's working on is worth a million dollars." Leila crossed her arms. "If you can sit there and tell me that *you* wouldn't have blown off a weekend with your girlfriend for a chance to earn a million bucks, then, yes, you're a better man than Elliot."

"There was one night," Simon mused, "when I would have given a million bucks to find my car keys. I had a Saturday-night date with Gloria, and I stayed a little too long. By the time I remembered I was meeting Susan for Sunday brunch, I couldn't find the keys to my car. What a mess."

"You would not have traded a million dollars for your car keys," Leila scoffed.

"Oh yes, I would. You didn't know Susan."

"No way." Leila shook her head in disbelief. "If someone had come up to you and said, 'Here's a million dollars. You can have that or your car keys,' you honestly expect me to believe you would have turned down the money?"

"Well, maybe not," Simon admitted. He scratched his head. "I guess there are a very few things someone would choose over a cool million bucks."

"That's rubbish," Marsh said evenly.

He'd been quiet for so long, Leila had almost forgotten he was standing there.

"I can think of dozens, right off the bat," he continued, sitting down across from her. "World peace. The end of hunger and starvation, a cure for cancer and AIDS. Shall I go on?"

"But that's all unrealistic," Leila protested. "Situations like that never arise. Sure, even Elliot would probably trade a million dollars for world peace. But he doesn't have to worry about it. He's never going to have to make that choice. It's theoretical."

Would Elliot trade a million dollars for anything? Leila wasn't absolutely positive. He'd grown up in a middle-class suburb of New York City, raised with the belief that money could buy the answer to any problem. He strove for, and achieved, the financial security his parents had never had. Money was his god and the monkey on his back. He both worshiped and cursed it, and no matter how much of it he had, he always wanted more.

Marsh, on the other hand, had been born with a silver spoon in his mouth. He had the attitude of the very wealthy. He'd always had money to burn, so he never hesitated to burn it. His lack of concern over financial matters had always infuriated Leila.

Marsh glanced at her as if he felt her studying him. His brown eyes were cool, his eyelids half-lowered as if he were relaxed, laid-back. Outside the window, on the beach, the quiet rush of the gentle Gulf waves murmured in the darkness.

"I'd gladly trade a million dollars," Marsh said quietly, "for one—just one—of my mother's smiles."

His gaze swept in Leila's direction, and this time he didn't look away. She suddenly realized that he wasn't relaxed at all. His eyelids were half-lowered to hide the inferno that was churning inside of him. She watched as Marsh leaned forward in his chair. In the bright overhead light, his angular face looked sharper, harsher, but no less handsome.

"I'd choose fertility for every couple in the world who want desperately to have a child," he continued. "I'd choose a brand new pair of legs that walk and run and jump, instead of that damned mechanical chair I ordered for little Billy Monroe. I'd choose life . . . or just another chance to save the life of every single patient I've lost in the ER." His voice shook slightly, and he stopped, looking down at the table in front of him. He took a deep breath, and when he spoke again his voice was steady.

"And if you want even more realistic choices, how about this: I'd choose the opportunity to live and work in the one place in the world I think of as my home, to have patients who are also my neighbors and friends, to know that when I walk down the street I'm respected and cared about by the people I pass. And yes, you're right, this was an actual choice I made several years ago. I turned down a job with a private practice in Boston that would have earned me quite a bit more than that million dollars by now. Down here on Sunrise Key, I may be living hand-to-mouth, but no one owns a piece of my soul." He smiled at Leila. "Perhaps my heart, but not my soul."

Leila was shocked. She hadn't known any of that. She'd never stopped to consider what Marsh had given up to live on Sunrise Key. And she'd never heard him speak so openly, so honestly. She hadn't realized he was capable of such heartfelt words.

Silence. Outside in the bushes, locusts chirped and whirred. On the beach, the waves continued their soft ebb and flow.

"Well," Marsh said with a soft laugh, "I certainly killed *that* conversation, didn't I?" He stood up, glancing at his watch. "It's getting late. I have to head over to the

Kavanaughs' to check on Kim and the baby once more before bed."

Marsh watched as Leila turned away and began straightening the papers on the dining room table. Well, that hadn't gone too badly. He'd said some things he never would have dared say to her before, and she hadn't run screaming from the room—or ridiculed him. She'd just stared at him in surprise, her eyes wide and violet blue and infinitely bottomless. He could have been pulled into her eyes and floated there for an eternity, and for several heart-stopping moments he had.

Do you want to come along to the Kavanaughs'? Marsh wanted to ask her, but he couldn't. It seemed a too blatantly obvious come-on. A moonlit night, a ride in Simon's jeep along the quiet island streets . . .

"I'm going upstairs," Leila announced, finally gathering up her notes. Her hair was charmingly rumpled, her blond curls mussed. "After I call Frankie, I'm going to bed." She gave both Marsh and Simon a long, hard look. "You guys say one word about this ninja thing to anyone, *anyone*, you're dead men. Got it?"

Simon and Marsh nodded solemnly.

That seemed to satisfy Leila. "See you in the morning."

"Good night," Marsh said. She turned to leave the room, but he had to stop her. "Leila?"

He hadn't been entirely honest. There was one more thing he would gladly trade a million dollars for.

She looked back at him, a question in her eyes.

"True love."

She frowned, clearly confused.

"I'd choose true love," Marsh said again, "over a million dollars. In fact, I'd trade a million dollars for even the mere hope of finding true love." He smiled at the look of sudden comprehension on her face. There was more, but he couldn't bring himself to say the words: *If I were Elliot, I wouldn't have stayed in New York this weekend. I would have gladly traded a million dollars to spend the weekend with you.*

She nodded. "Good night," she murmured.

As she left the room, he turned to find Simon watching him.

"I'm dying to see where this is going to go," Simon said.

Marsh took a deep breath, letting it slowly out. "I'm just dying."

FOUR

"Going to the beach?" Marsh asked as he came into the kitchen and poured himself a cup of coffee. Bright morning sunlight streamed in through the window.

Leila was wearing a short filmy sundress over her bathing suit. It was a two piece, in a bright blue-and-green pattern that was clearly visible underneath the white, gauzy fabric of her dress.

"Good guess," she said, then drained her glass of juice.

"Simon up yet?" He leaned against the kitchen counter as he looked at Leila over the edge of his coffee cup.

Leila shot him a look, implying that his question was a ridiculous one.

"Right," Marsh said. "He's still asleep."

She turned to pick up her beach bag and a towel.

"Mind if I tag along?" Marsh asked. "You know, to the beach?"

Surprised, Leila turned to look at him. He was wearing his bathing suit, too, she realized. Funny, she'd just assumed he'd be going in to his office.

"I'm taking some time off," he told her, as if he could read her mind. "Of course, I'm on call for emergencies, but I'm taking the next few weeks easy. I have no scheduled appointments today. Tomorrow I'm only going in for a half day, and the day after I'm off again."

He was watching her, and his eyes were positively warm. In fact, Leila felt if she looked at him for too long, she just might spontaneously combust.

"That's . . . nice," she said.

His bathing suit was neon orange with a funky black pattern. It had to be one of Simon's since most of Marsh's clothes had been destroyed in the fire, she remembered. Still, it looked good on him. It was short and showed off his long, muscular, tanned legs. He had nice legs—and she was staring at them, she realized suddenly.

She glanced up into his face again, only to find that his eyes were taking their own leisurely stroll up and down her legs.

Leila turned away, afraid he would see the expression on her face. She knew that she couldn't hide the sudden wave of longing she felt—or the surprise she felt at the odd sensation of wanting.

That ninja and his high-voltage kisses had really thrown her emotions out of whack. If she was driven to staring at Marsh Devlin's legs—nice as they might be— she was in worse shape than she'd thought.

Taking a deep, cleansing breath, Leila led the way down the steps from the deck and onto the beach. The sand was warm and felt delicious beneath her bare toes. She stopped walking to luxuriate in the sensation. Boy, she loved it there on Sunrise Key's gorgeous beach.

Seabirds danced and floated on the cool breeze that was coming in directly off the sparkling blue-green Gulf water. The sky was the perfect shade of blue, with puffy white clouds that looked as if they had been drawn there. Sunlight was reflecting off the pure white sand.

"It's so beautiful here," she said with a sigh. "Like paradise."

Marsh nodded. He was watching her again.

"Did you really turn down a high-paying job in Boston in order to live here?"

He drew a line in the sand with his toe. "Is that really so strange?"

"How could you just turn your back on all that money?"

"How could I not?"

Leila stared out at the ocean, more affected than she would have thought possible by the simplicity of his answer.

"The people I care most about in the world all live down here," Marsh said. "Well, most of them, anyway. And like you said, it's paradise."

Leila still didn't speak, didn't move.

"Besides," Marsh continued. "Six-figure salaries are way overrated."

She looked at him then. "You still believe that? Even though you're currently living hand-to-mouth?"

Marsh winced. "Ah, yes. I *did* mention something about that last night, didn't I?"

"Simon says your account books are a mess. Will you let me take a look at them?"

"You're supposed to be on vacation," Marsh said.

"You're helping me with my wild goose chase." She started walking again, heading across the wide beach toward the lounge chairs that were near the edge of the water. "Let me help you, too."

"I don't think this is a wild goose chase." Marsh followed her. "You know, finding your ninja. I think it's a good idea."

"You do." The sea breeze lifted the edge of her skirt, and Marsh's eyes followed.

"I'd just like to know one thing. Have you thought any more about what you intend to do if you actually find him?"

"Best-case scenario?" Leila asked, and he nodded. "With any luck, he'll be awful, and that'll burst the whole fantasy bubble. Then I can get on with my life."

"Marry Elliot, in other words."

"Yeah," Leila said. "Maybe I'll marry Elliot."

Marsh was silent for a moment, and all Leila could hear was the sound their feet made in the sand.

"What if the bubble *isn't* burst?" he asked. "What then?"

Leila shook her head. "I'm still not sure," she admitted.

"Come on. What's the best-case scenario if your ninja *isn't* awful?" Marsh persisted.

"You mean, if he's perfect?" Leila smiled. "He's perfect, he's madly in love with me, and he asks me—on the spot—to marry him. I, of course, accept, recognizing my true destiny when I see it."

Marsh frowned slightly. "What if . . ." He cleared his throat. "What if he's not *truly* perfect? I mean, what if he's slightly less than perfect? Well, no, what I really mean is, what if he's a whole lot less than perfect, but he still loves you madly, and all that? I mean, no one's ever truly perfect. . . ."

"What I meant was, if he's perfect *for me*." Leila put her bag on one of the lounge chairs. "You're extremely interested in all this, aren't you?"

"I'm concerned you'll do something that you'll end up regretting."

Leila pulled her sundress over her head. "Well, that's sweet, but I seriously doubt that finding this ninja is something I'm going to regret."

"I meant marrying Elliot."

He was watching her again, and Leila checked her bathing suit to make sure it was covering everything it was supposed to. Of course, there was nothing she had that he hadn't already seen. He was a doctor, for crying out loud. Still, the look in his eyes was appreciative and extremely male.

"You look terrific," Marsh said. "New suit?"

"Thanks." Leila sat down on her chair and fished through her beach bag for her sunglasses and sunblock. "Yeah, it's new."

"I like it." His approval warmed his already rich voice.

It was odd, but Leila couldn't remember the last time she'd been to the beach with Marsh. She'd been returning to the island just about every six months or so for years and years—there must've been at least one time they both went to the beach and . . .

Marsh sat down in the other chair and pulled off his T-shirt. And Leila knew for certain that she hadn't been to the beach with him in a very long time. Probably not since he was in college and she was in high school. Because she remembered him as a skinny kid, all ribs and shoulder blades and collarbones and elbows. But the person sitting next to her was neither skinny nor a kid. He was a man. He had muscles—tan, smooth, well-defined muscles. He even had hair on his chest.

Marsh took a pair of round mirror-lensed sunglasses from his fanny pack and put them on. His hair was a mess from pulling his shirt over his head, and the ocean breeze made it dance charmingly around his face, blowing a stray lock into his eyes and then sweeping it away. He smiled at her, one of his rare, relaxed grins, and the combination made him look about as much unlike the Marshall Devlin she thought she knew as possible. In fact, he looked like the kind of guy that, if she saw him across the room at a party, she'd pressure her host into introducing to her. His gaze locked with hers over the top of his sunglasses. Instant heat.

"Mind if I borrow your sunblock?" She handed him the bottle. His fingers brushed hers and she nearly dropped it, shocked by the sudden sensation of electricity. What was going on?

"Why aren't you married?" she asked him, suddenly.

"Well, you lost me there. Usually I can follow your

insane conversational tangents, but this one got away from me."

"You're a good-looking man," Leila said bluntly. "On top of that, you're a doctor. So why hasn't some smart woman hooked you and reeled you in, like some giant, prize catch?"

"Good Lord, you make it sound so appealing."

"I know why Simon isn't married," Leila said. "It's because he's still a child. And as long as he can manage to attract his sweet-young-things-du-jour, he's never going to settle down. But you're the type of guy who wants the whole package, you know, wife and kids, two-car garage, Irish setter named Sparky. . . . ?"

Marsh carefully applied sunblock to his shoulders and neck. Leila had the feeling that he was deciding how much—or which version—of the truth to tell her.

"You're right. I want all that. I'm just not thoroughly convinced that it's an attainable goal." He looked out at the water, squinting despite his sunglasses. "I don't know how much you know about me," he added, glancing back at Leila, "but when I was about six, my parents went through a divorce. It was . . . bad."

My God, Leila realized. He was telling her the truth. He was actually opening up—a little—to her.

He looked at her again. "Actually, it wasn't bad, it was bloody awful. My mother was nearly destroyed. I don't think she ever really recovered. And I couldn't figure out what went wrong." He shook his head. "Up to the point they split up, they seemed so much in love. But they couldn't make it work."

Leila didn't know whether to stay silent and hope

that he continued talking, or to urge him to tell her more. He was quiet for so long, she finally spoke. "I know divorce statistics are high, but some people still have marriages that last. It's not impossible, Marsh."

He took off his sunglasses and rubbed his eyes. "I just keep thinking, if my parents couldn't do it, how can I?"

"Because you're not your parents."

"Thank goodness for that." Marsh smiled at her. It was a rueful smile, but still it made her feel as if the laws of gravity were temporarily suspended.

"Yo, Marsh!"

Leila and Marsh looked up to see Simon jogging toward them from the house. "Ben Sullivan just called. He needs you out at his place pronto. He's got an emergency."

"Human or other?" Marsh asked, already pulling on his T-shirt.

"Other." Simon's hair was standing straight up and he wore only a colorful pair of boxer shorts. It was clear he'd rolled directly out of bed to deliver this message. "One of his broodmares has the worst case of colic he's ever seen. He apologized all over the place for interrupting your vacation, but he's tried everything, and he's desperate. I told him you'd be right there."

"Care to come along for the ride?" Marsh asked Leila as he slipped his feet into his sneakers.

"It depends," she said dryly. "Are we going to start arguing about having the windows up or down the minute I get into your car?"

"My car was in the garage under the house when it burned."

"Oh, *no.*" Leila cringed.

"Oh, yes. I rode my bike in to the office that day. I've been borrowing Simon's jeep until the insurance money comes through. The jeep has no doors, therefore it has no windows, and nothing we can argue about. If we get desperate, I suppose we could argue about which radio station to listen to."

"Let me grab a pair of shorts and my sneakers," Leila said.

"You're going?" Simon asked. "With *Dev?*" Simon looked surprised.

Marsh looked impatient. He grabbed Leila by the shoulders and gently pushed her toward the house.

"Hurry. Get your things. I'll be out front."

Why *was* she going to the Sullivan's with Marsh? Simon was still staring at her as if she'd undergone some kind of bizarre personality change. "It's been ages since I've seen Nancy Sullivan," Leila explained.

"Go," Marsh said.

She went.

Leila leaned against the rough-hewn door to the big barn, watching Marsh examine Ben Sullivan's mare.

The horse was clearly in agony, but Marsh touched it gently, talking to it in a calm, soothing voice.

"Gee, I wish he'd talk to *me* like that," Nancy Sullivan said, coming up behind her. "But no, the man's a walking ice cube. It's that British chilliness, you know?"

"Hey, there you are." Leila smiled. "Your brother said you were around here somewhere."

"That's me. Always around here somewhere. Long time, no see, stranger."

"Yeah, it's been at least a year," Leila said. "You look great. How are you?"

In the barn, Marsh and Ben stripped off their T-shirts and kicked off their sneakers.

"Uh-oh." Nancy pulled Leila out into the yard. "They're going for the hose. This is *not* going to be pretty . . . despite Dr. Devlin's obvious physical attributes. Is that man gorgeous, or what?"

Leila looked at Marsh, trying to see him through Nancy's eyes. He *was* gorgeous, with all that tanned skin and those gleaming muscles. But what had Nancy said about him—he was a walking ice cube? Two days ago, Leila would have agreed. But lately he seemed to be 100 percent hot-blooded. Was it possible that the fire that burned down his house had somehow thawed him out? Or was she simply seeing him in a different light?

"Let's get out of here before they ask us to help." Nancy tugged at her arm.

"What are they gonna do?"

Briefly, Nancy ran down the medical procedure for relieving the mare's colic, and Leila's eyes widened.

"That doesn't sound like much fun for the horse *or* the doctor." She glanced into the barn. Since when did Marsh get down in the dust and dirt—soon to be mud, what with the water from the hose—while he played Dr. Dolittle to an equine patient? This was a man who had graduated at the top of his class from Harvard Medical School.

He was also, apparently, a man who got more value from helping his friends—one of whom was Ben Sullivan—than from earning scads of money.

"Let's make some lemonade," Nancy suggested. "Something tells me Ben and Marsh are going to need it when this is over."

"Lemonade . . . and a shower." Leila followed her friend into the kitchen, unable to keep from looking back over her shoulder at the barn.

"So are you and the good doctor an item these days?" Nancy asked casually as she took a bag of lemons from the refrigerator.

She and Marsh? An item? "Oh, no," Leila said hastily. "No, no. He's staying up at our house. You know, since the fire?"

"Yeah, that was a shame, huh? I heard he lost everything, even his car. Grab a knife and help me with these, will you?"

Obediently, Leila began slicing the lemons that Nancy washed and put out on the cutting board.

"I also heard," Nancy continued, "that Marsh's homeowner's insurance won't cover the cost of rebuilding his place. There's some legal glitch. He's about fifty thousand short."

"That can't be right."

"You're the math expert," Nancy said. "You should talk to Marsh about it. Apparently, on top of everything else, he's having trouble getting a loan for that fifty thousand from the bank. Ever since our little savings and loan got bought out by that big corporate bank, people are getting turned down for loans left and right. Can you imagine? The town *doctor* refused a mortgage because he's not solvent enough." She was silent for a moment, shaking her head. "Let me tell you, there's hardly anyone in town who doesn't owe Marshall Devlin money. If he called in all of his loans and got tough with his accounts receivable, he'd be solvent enough, believe me. But he'll never do that. Not while times are so tough."

Nancy started talking about the Kavanaugh's new baby, but Leila's mind was still on Marsh. Simon had hinted that Marsh's books needed an overhaul, but he hadn't said anything about problems with the insurance company or loans being turned down by the bank. That was bad. That was *really* bad. If he needed help, why hadn't he simply asked?

The sound of the outside shower going on caught Nancy's attention, and she put the pitcher of lemonade and four tall glasses on a tray. "Grab a couple of towels from the hall closet," she ordered Leila as she carried the tray out onto the wide, wraparound porch.

The screen door squeaked as Leila pushed it open. She walked across the dusty drive to the outside of the barn, carrying two thick towels in her arms. Marsh was standing under an outdoor spigot, letting the water cascade over his head.

He stood back slightly, pushing the hair out of his eyes and caught sight of Leila watching him. He smiled a greeting.

"Is the mare okay?"

"She's not too happy with us right now." Marsh let

the water rinse the rest of the mud and muck from his body. "But I think she's feeling a little better."

He shut off the faucet and wiped the water from his hair and face with his hands. Leila held out one of the towels, but he didn't take it right away. He stood for a moment and dripped, smiling at her.

Standing there with sparkling beads of water running from his hair down his broad shoulders and strong, muscular arms, it was easy to see why Nancy Sullivan found Marsh so attractive. He *was* attractive. But even more attractive than his obvious physical attributes was his intense pleasure at a job well done. As unpleasant as treating a horse with colic might be, Marsh truly enjoyed the fact that he'd been able to help.

"I don't know you very well at all, do I?" Leila said as he finally took the towel from her hands.

He was drying his face, but her words made him pause and look up at her.

"I had no idea you subbed for the veterinarian when he was off the island." Leila hung the second towel on a hook near the shower.

"The local vet retired two years ago. If the vet from the mainland can't get over here—and he usually can't, it's a three-hour round-trip for him—I'm the closest thing to a vet there is on Sunrise Key."

"And you've been doing this for two *years?*"

Marsh smiled. "I'm pretty good with horses and dogs. Chickens and pigs, however, continue to be something of a challenge."

"I'm amazed," Leila said.

"I've actually taken a few of those college courses in

veterinary medicine. You know, the courses that link you to the professor via cable television. It's fascinating stuff, Leila. And I truly love working with the horses—even at times like this, when it can get rather nasty. Say, did you know I've learned to ride?"

"No."

"It's indescribable. Incredible. Riding on the beach, it's like flying, only better." He smiled sheepishly as he dried the back of his neck with the towel. "You probably think I've gone absolutely mad."

"No, I don't." Leila laughed, shaking her head. "I'm just surprised. I didn't think you got this passionate about *anything*."

Marsh's smile faded and he turned slightly away from her.

"I didn't mean—"

"Yes, you did mean it." His voice was gentle, contradicting the harshness of his words. "But like you said, you don't know me very well."

Embarrassed, Leila looked down at the puddle of water that would surely evaporate quickly in the warm sunshine. "I'm sorry," she said.

He touched her gently underneath her chin, lifting her head so that she was looking directly into his eyes.

"The fact is, there're quite a few things I'm passionate about. Riding horses, delivering healthy babies, good salsa music, my American grandmother's chocolate chip cookies, old Hitchcock movies, making love . . ." His gaze dropped languidly to Leila's mouth. "Especially making love."

He looked back into Leila's eyes and she knew he

was going to kiss her. Her heart flipped in her chest as he leaned closer—

"Ready for a glass of lemonade, y'all?" Ben Sullivan asked, coming out of the barn. "I'll join you on the porch, after I hose down here. Stand aside, Doc, and let me get under this shower."

Marsh let go of Leila, and she quickly turned away, heading for the porch and Nancy—and safety.

Oh, God, had she actually almost kissed Marsh Devlin? She and Marsh argued and fought. They didn't talk about personal things like passion and making love, and they sure as hell didn't *kiss*. Sure, sparks flew when they were together, but they were sparks that flared and burned out quickly, before catching fire. So why did it seem that lately all she had to do was exchange a single glance with Marsh, and the entire world was in danger of going up in flames?

All of this business with the mystery ninja must be setting her off balance.

As for Marsh, well, no doubt he was in a current low spot in his life, too. His home had just burned to the ground and he'd lost nearly everything he owned, some of it irreplaceable. To top it off, he was in a financial bind. He was overworked and tired. He had to be depressed, as well as lonely. He was looking for a little comfort, Leila told herself firmly. In his situation, who wouldn't be?

The drive back into town was filled with tension. Marsh had spent the past half hour at the Sullivan's sipping lemonade and alternately cursing and thanking God for Ben's incredible timing.

Lord, but he wanted to kiss Leila again. Kissing Leila was heaven, and he wanted another glimpse of that paradise. Though he knew kissing her would make him only want more. He wanted to make love to her. He wanted to show her, firsthand, just how passionate he could be.

Her words still stung. She had honestly thought he was cold and hard-hearted. Marsh wasn't like Simon, it was true. Marsh wasn't the type who turned cartwheels of joy at the drop of a hat. He was more careful about what he allowed the world to witness. With the sole exception of bursts of his too hot temper, Marsh was cautious about letting his feelings control him. But that didn't mean those feelings weren't there.

One kiss, he thought, glancing at Leila in the passenger seat. That's all it would take. He could pull the jeep over to the side of the road, take her in his arms, and kiss her. Then she would know that the blood that flowed through his veins was hot. She would also know that he was the man who had kissed her as the clock struck midnight, as the New Year dawned.

And then she would have a heart attack, and run screaming from the jeep, away from him, Marsh thought wryly. Leila was starting to like him, but she wasn't ready to be told that he was the man she was searching for. She had to find that out for herself. Marsh had to take this slowly, or risk frightening her away.

"How well do you know the Sullivans?" Leila asked, breaking the silence.

Marsh looked at her in surprise. "Not all that well.

They're down here with their horses every winter. I suppose I don't know them as well as the people who live here year-round, though I consider Ben a man to be trusted. Why do you ask?"

Leila smiled at him. "I think Nancy has a crush on you."

"Nancy Sullivan." Marsh carefully hid his surprise. Why was Leila telling him this?

"I was thinking." Leila glanced at him from the corners of her eyes. "How about if I invite Nancy over to dinner one of these nights and—"

Marsh hit the brakes hard and the jeep squealed to a stop. Good God, she was trying to set him up with her friend. "You can't be serious."

"She's nice, Marsh. I think if you get to know her, you'll like her—"

"I'm not interested in Nancy Sullivan."

"How do you know, when you just told me that you don't know her very well?" Leila countered.

"If I wanted to ask Nancy Sullivan out, I would have done so already myself," Marsh said through tightly clenched teeth. Lord, this was an amazingly ludicrous conversation. Less than an hour ago, he'd come damn close to kissing this woman. They'd both been well aware of the undercurrents in the air. Dammit, Leila knew he was going to kiss her, and she hadn't backed away. If Ben hadn't interrupted them, he *would* have kissed her. So why was she trying to pair him off with one of her friends now?

"Will you lighten up?" Leila said. "God, you'd think

I was trying to arrange for your execution. I'm trying to help, and you fly into one of your awful snits."

"You're trying to help? What, pray tell, are you trying to help me do, exactly? Get married? Settle down? Have a houseful of kids? Or is it more basic than that? Perhaps you're only trying to help me get laid."

Silence. There was silence in the jeep as Leila stared out the windshield and Marsh cursed his bloody temper.

"I'm sorry." He raked his fingers through his hair.

"No, you're right. I was butting in. *I'm* sorry."

She glanced over at him, and he saw that there were tears in her eyes. For a moment, he had trouble catching his breath, as if someone had knocked all of the air out of him.

"Oh, Leila, I didn't mean to say that—"

"Forget it." She wouldn't meet his eyes. "We fight all the time."

"Not like that. I shouldn't have said that."

She got out of the jeep. "I'm going to walk over to Frankie's."

Marsh pulled himself up so that he was standing on the running board, looking at her over the canvas top of the jeep. "Leila, wait, please. I'm sorry—"

"I said, forget it."

His temper flared. "Dammit, will you let me properly apologize?"

"Why? Will that make you feel better?"

She spun back to face him, and he saw that anger had replaced the tears in her eyes. Anger was better than hurt, but not by much. His hair was in his eyes again, he realized, and he wearily pushed it back, off his face.

"No," he said quietly.

To his surprise, Leila didn't turn and walk away. Instead, she stepped closer to the jeep. "Things are a real mess, aren't they, Marsh? In both of our lives."

"It's true that my house burning down has been rather . . . inconvenient, but it's just a matter of time before . . ."

"What? Before you rebuild?"

"Well, yes."

"That's not what I hear," she said. "Not with the problems you're having with your insurance company. Not with the bank loan you can't seem to qualify for."

Marsh ran his hands across his face. "Ah, the drawback of small-town life. Secrets aren't secret for long, are they? As you're fond of pointing out every chance you get."

"I want to help you get your financial situation on track." Leila took another step toward him. She looked lovely in the early afternoon light. The sun made her golden hair shine. And her face . . . God, he'd dreamed about her beautiful smile, her eyes dancing with pleasure and laughter. He'd fantasized about holding her in his arms. "Let me look at your books."

"It's an improvement over helping me get my love life on track, but not by too much."

"Don't go all macho and stupid on me, Devlin." Leila narrowed her eyes. "You've never been able to balance even your checkbook, and you know it. This isn't a matter of manly pride."

"Believe me, you stomped the last tattered pieces of my manly pride firmly into the ground with that bit about Nancy Sullivan," Marsh said ruefully. "I'd much rather we'd just drop this whole conversation. Let me drive you to Frankie's and we'll pretend it never happened."

Leila was silent, staring down at the dusty pavement, out at the overgrown junglelike bushes that lined the road, up at the crystal blue of the sky. Finally she looked back at Marsh. "I can't just let it go, Marshall. You'd think I would be able to, after all the years we've fought and argued and just in general pretended to dislike each other. But I'm not sure if you changed or I changed or what, but I . . . I *do* care about you, and I need you to let me help you."

Marsh stood quietly and let her words digest. She *cared* about him. It was a step in the right direction. Not a big step, but a step.

He nodded. "All right. You win."

"Good."

"Just the financial stuff," Marsh added. "Not the other."

Leila climbed into the jeep and fastened her seat belt. "In other words, if you want to get laid, you'll do it without my help."

She was intentionally trying to embarrass him. But it wouldn't work.

"Without your help as my social director," Marsh corrected her, giving her a sidelong glance. "Anytime you're interested in a different . . . position, I'd be more than happy to oblige."

Leila's eyes widened as she realized the double meaning of his words.

"Haven't you ever wondered what it would be like, Leila—you know, you and me?"

His words brought the flush of heat to Leila's cheeks as she tried to look away, as she tried to keep from getting caught in the depths of his eyes.

A supernova. That's what it would be like. An explosion of incredible, unending, unstoppable heat. Arms and legs and bodies and mouths entangled in an almost painful need to be one. He would devour her, even as she consumed him. . . .

"No," she lied, trying desperately to keep her voice from sounding so breathless. "No, actually I haven't."

All of the warmth left his eyes, leaving only a trace of disappointment that was quickly hidden beneath his usual mocking glint.

"Right," he said briskly. "That's the trouble with you accountants. No imagination. Everything's facts and figures."

Leila kept her mouth shut as Marsh started the jeep with a roar of the engine.

They drove to Frankie's office in silence.

FIVE

Preston Seaholm, Hayden Young, and Liam Halliday had each attended Simon's party dressed in a ninja costume. All three also owned a beeper. Hayden had one because along with his lifeguard job, he moonlighted as a paramedic and volunteer fireman. Liam was the sheriff, and as everybody knew, there were times—like when Duke Torrelson had too much tequila and jumped on top of the jukebox in the Rustler's Hideout and challenged everyone in the place to a leg-wrestling match—when the mere deputies simply couldn't cut it. And Preston had a beeper because, according to Frankie, he was pretentious.

Leila stared at the list of six names she'd given Frankie to check out.

From those six names, she had narrowed her suspects down to three. Three men, three beepers, three ninjas.

Except, Marsh and Simon—and Frankie, too—had spotted a *fourth* ninja at the New Year's Eve party.

And that was probably the mysterious Robert Earle.

Frankie had checked into Alan Lanigan and Bruce Kimble, both longtime residents of Sunrise Key, the other two names on the list. She had found that Alan hadn't even attended the party and that Bruce had come dressed as Godzilla.

But Robert Earle had been a visitor to the key. He'd been staying at Seaholm's resort and had checked out early in the afternoon of January first. Frankie hadn't managed to persuade the hotel clerk to give her Earle's home address, so she hadn't been able to track the man any further. As a result, Leila didn't know a thing about him, whether he owned a beeper, whether he wore a ninja costume to the party. Or whether he was her mystery man.

Leila had asked Simon about Robert Earle, but he wasn't any help. Apparently, he'd met Earle on the golf course, the two men had hit it off, and Simon had invited him to the party. He thought Earle lived up in Georgia. Atlanta, maybe.

Frankie had promised to get Earle's home address from the resort one way or another. Leila didn't dare ask how.

But for now she had three names, three suspects, three places to start.

Frankie had told her that Pres Seaholm, the first suspected ninja, could usually be found down at his various construction sites, or at the marina where he docked his yacht. Occasionally he could be found at his office, which was on Ocean Avenue, in the same building as Marsh's office.

It was still funny to think that Marsh was a doctor, even though he'd been practicing for years. Leila had never gone to see him as a patient. It was hard to imagine him giving her any kind of examination, even something as simple as looking at a sore throat. Of course, she'd been lucky. She'd never gotten sick or been hurt while here on vacation.

She could just picture him, calm and aloof and in control while she nearly wept aloud from intense pain.

Or maybe not. Over the past few days, she'd seen a new side of Marsh. He wasn't as calm and self-confident as she'd always thought. He doubted his ability to make a marriage work. He was afraid of being hurt the way his mother had been. He was vulnerable, and capable of feeling pain. He was neither icy hearted nor emotionless. . . .

What was she doing? She was supposed to be figuring out which of her suspects to approach first, not thinking about Marsh Devlin.

Hayden Young. She should be thinking about Hayden Young instead. The new lifeguard lived not far from the town beach, where he spent most of the hours from sunrise to sunset. She should be thinking about the best way to introduce herself to Hayden Young, instead of daydreaming about Marsh Devlin.

Except it was hard *not* to think about Marsh. *Have you ever wondered what it would be like, Leila . . . you know, you and me?* Had he known she was lying when she told him no? What if she had said yes? Yes, she *had* wondered, and lately it seemed as if she was wondering all the time. Would he have kissed her if she'd admitted the truth? And what about at the Sullivan's? If Ben hadn't come out of the barn, would he have kissed her then?

This was really stupid. She *had* to stop thinking about Marsh. Leila frowned down at her list of names.

Liam Halliday.

Liam was the town sheriff. He was a little bit harder to pinpoint than the other two men, except on his rare nights off. Then, according to Frankie, you could find him, without fail, at the Rustler's Hideout, drinking beer, shooting pool, and dancing the two-step to the country songs on the jukebox.

And tonight was one of Liam's nights off. There was no telling when he'd have another night free.

So it was Liam she'd go to see first. It was Liam she'd try to kiss.

Too bad it couldn't have been Marsh.

Leila was sitting drowsily in the sun out on the deck when a voice made her open her eyes.

"I heard rumors you were back in town."

It was Preston Seaholm, one of her ninja suspects, and he was leaning against the deck railing, smoking a cigarette. He was wearing a cranberry-colored polo shirt and a pair of expensive-looking black shorts. His reddish-blond hair was growing long in the back, and he had a heavy five-o'clock shadow, as if he hadn't shaved in days. It made him look faintly dangerous.

"I heard rumors *you* were back in town, too. It's been a long time. How are you?"

He smiled very slightly and took the last drag on his cigarette, stubbing it out in an ashtray that sat on the railing. "Unmarried." He exhaled the smoke. There might have been a flash of pain in his hazel eyes, but if there was, it was gone as quickly as it had appeared. "No doubt you heard *those* rumors, too."

"I've heard a few," Leila admitted. Was Pres Seaholm her ninja? She looked into his eyes, searching for some kind of sign, some kind of recognition.

"Is Simon around?" Pres asked. "I'm in the market for some Stickley furniture, and rumor has it—there go those rumors again—he's got a lead on an entire house-ful."

"He's in his office. I'll walk you back there." She sat up and started to pull herself to her feet. This was the perfect opportunity. But for what? How on earth was she going to get him to kiss her?

"I know the way," he said. "Don't get up."

"That's okay." She slipped her sundress over her bathing suit. "Actually, I want to ask you—"

Standing there, face-to-face—or nose to nose, as it were—Leila knew she didn't have to kiss Pres Seaholm to convince herself that he wasn't her ninja. Because her ninja wasn't a smoker. Her ninja hadn't smelled—or tasted—of cigarettes. Pres did. Everything about him reeked of tobacco smoke.

"I wanted to ask you," Leila said, filled with relief that she didn't have to make a fool of herself, "about that building that you're putting up over by the airport." She led him into the house. "Nobody I've talked to seems to know. Is it going to be a restaurant or some kind of store . . . ?"

Midafternoon, Frankie called.

"Robert Earle." She skipped the hellos.

"Did you find out something?" Leila asked.

"He's a skeeve. I, um, located his home address and gave him a call. *Mrs.* Earle answered the phone."

"Uh-oh."

"Uh-oh's right," Frankie agreed. "And Mrs. Earle didn't have a clue that her husband had spent a week on Sunrise Key. She was under the impression that he'd been attending some kind of corporate convention in Orlando. I didn't try to correct her poor deluded view of reality. I told her I must be mistaken and left it at that. You want me to pursue it, try to get his work number?"

Leila lay back on her bed. "No." She stared up at the ceiling. "Let me check out Liam Halliday and Hayden Young first."

"Have we already disqualified Pres Seaholm?" Frankie asked.

"He smokes like a chimney. You can't get within six feet of him without smelling tar and nicotine. The man's a walking ashtray. He's *not* my ninja."

"So, one down," Frankie said. "That's good news, provided that your ninja's *not* being a billionaire is good news."

Leila laughed. "Right."

"I'll see you tonight," Frankie said. "For Operation Halliday."

"I'm going out with Frankie tonight," Leila announced as dinner was drawing to a close. "We're going over to the Rustler's Hideout."

Both Marsh and Simon eyed her speculatively. In both pairs of eyes she could read only one thing: Liam Halliday. She never should have told them that Frankie had narrowed down the list of possible ninjas to Liam, Pres, and Hayden.

"Gonna do some line dancing, huh?" Simon said, a knowing glint in his eyes. "Put on your cowboy boots and do some boot scootin'?" He looked at Marsh and grinned. "You know who I hear is a really good dancer? Liam Halliday. Can you believe it? For such a tall guy, he can really shake a leg."

"Knock it off, Si," Leila said tightly.

"We can't let Leila go alone," Simon told Marsh.

"I suppose you're right," Marsh mused. "The Rustler's Hideout is no place for a lady to go by herself."

"I'm *not* going alone. I'm going with *Frankie*. You two are *not* invited."

"Frankie's barely five feet tall," Simon remarked.

"She won't be extremely useful if Duke has one of his flashbacks and starts swinging his pool cue around like a wild man," Marsh admitted.

"I hear Duke's meeting his biker buddies at the Hideout tonight," Simon said. "They're a pretty scary gang."

"Everyone knows that Duke's a pussycat," Leila protested. "His so-called biker friends ride Schwinns. Frankie and I will be fine—"

"Still, maybe we should go, too," Simon said. "I'm not doing anything tonight. You're not busy either, are you, Dev?"

"No." Leila stood up, carrying her plate into the kitchen. "Absolutely not."

They wanted to tag along. They wanted to watch her approach Liam Halliday, to see if he was her ninja. They wanted to witness her making an ass of herself.

"My schedule's clear, too," Marsh said cheerfully, as both he and Simon followed her into the kitchen.

"Nope," Leila insisted. "You're not coming. No way."

Simon smiled. "I'll drive."

"I think you should ask him to dance," Frankie told Leila.

"No," Simon said "Fall to the floor and act like you need mouth-to-mouth resuscitation. That'll do it. Liam'll be over here in a flash."

"Marsh is here," Frankie drawled scornfully. "You don't really think the sheriff's going to resuscitate Leila when the town doctor is standing two feet away from her, do you?"

"Good point," Marsh said.

"Maybe if Marsh went into the men's room first . . ." Simon started.

"No resuscitation," Leila said firmly. "No, thank you."

"Then just walk up to him and plant one on him," Simon suggested. "It'll blow his mind, but it'll get the job done."

"I *still* think you should ask him to dance," Frankie said. "Then you can just let nature take its course. Two minutes into the dance, *he'll* be the one trying to figure out how to get *you* to kiss *him*."

The Rustler's Hideout was fairly busy for a weeknight. Although the bandstand was empty, the jukebox was playing, and seven or eight couples moved around the little dance floor.

The air was smoky and the lights were dim, and other than a promotional picture of Clint Black that had recently been tacked up on the rough-hewn walls, Leila didn't think the bar had changed one bit since she was last there, four years before. It was not that the tiny roadhouse wasn't clean, because it was. The place had an obviously well-cared-for appearance. Yet it held a sense of timelessness. When she opened the door and walked inside, it could've been 1985. Or 1975. Or even 1955. Only the songs playing on the jukebox were different.

Leila leaned on the rail that separated the dance floor from the rest of the bar. Frankie was next to her, and Marsh and Simon were nearby. She could see Liam Halliday, across the room, sitting alone at the long, worn, wooden bar.

Even from the back, the sheriff of Sunrise Key was good-looking. His hair was thick and dark and it curled over the collar of his blue chambray shirt. He was resting his elbows against the bar, and that pulled the fabric of his shirt tightly across his broad shoulders and muscular back. The shirt was tucked neatly into a snug-fitting pair of jeans so faded they were almost white. He wore cowboy boots. Leila could see the chains of his boot bracelets gleaming in the darkness.

"How well do you know him?" Leila asked Frankie. "Could you introduce us?"

"Well, yeah. But that might not be such a good idea. He's not my biggest fan these days. He's a little annoyed that I've got my PI license. He thinks all I really want to do is dress up like Humphrey Bogart in *The Maltese Falcon* and play pretend."

Leila glanced at Simon who at least had the good grace to look uncomfortable. He'd said nearly the exact same thing about Frankie's PI license.

"That's why he gave me that job digging through the dumpster," Frankie continued. "He thought I'd turn it down. Well, I didn't, and now he's madder than ever."

Simon cleared his throat. "I don't know Halliday that well, but I can introduce you to him, if you really want, Lei."

Leila made a face. "No, that would be too weird. What would you say? 'Hi, meet my sister, she wants to kiss you?'"

"That wasn't what I had in mind."

"The bar stool next to the sheriff's is empty," Frankie said. "Go sit down next to him, order a beer, and see what happens. You've got to do *something*."

"You might consider telling him the truth." Marsh spoke up for the first time in a long while.

Tell Liam the truth?

Leila looked at Marsh. He was leaning against a support pole, his hands jammed into the front pockets of his jeans. . . . Jeans? Yes, he was actually wearing jeans. They weren't as faded as the pair Liam Halliday was wearing, but they looked as if they'd feel soft to the touch. His shirt was one of his regular old white cotton button-downs. As usual, the top few buttons were undone, and he'd rolled the sleeves up to his elbows. It, too, was worn—the collar was starting to fray.

The sight of that fraying collar gave Leila a shock. Funny, but she'd always thought of Marsh as an extremely well-to-do type who'd refuse to wear anything but a crisp, new, professionally laundered shirt. But he'd carried himself with that air of quiet wealth for so long, it was possible that his shirts had been frayed for years, and Leila simply hadn't noticed.

His brown eyes were bemused as he watched her study him so seriously, so intently.

"The truth," she echoed. "You mean, tell him . . ."

"Everything," Marsh finished. "The whole story. The Cinderella costume, the clock striking midnight, the vanishing ninja . . ."

"The kiss," Leila said.

"Yes." Their gazes locked, and for one brief moment the music, the dancers, Simon and Frankie, the entire bar seemed to disappear. For one brief moment, Marsh and his warm brown eyes were all that existed, and Leila had the odd sensation of flying, of weightlessness, of stomach-flipping freefall.

"No way." Simon jostled her, bringing her back to reality. The music blared, suddenly seeming way too loud, and Leila lost her balance. "You can't tell him the truth. It sounds like you're nuts. He'll think you're making it all up and he'll back away."

Simon didn't seem to notice when Leila swayed, but Marsh was there, steadying her by holding her elbow. His fingers were warm and solid against the bare skin of her arm.

"You all right?" he murmured, and she nodded. But he didn't let go of her, and she was oddly glad.

"It *is* a pretty strange story." Frankie agreed with Simon for once. "On the other hand, you don't want to put yourself into a situation where you're leading Liam on. Because if you're wrong, and he wasn't the one you're looking for, it'll be really difficult to discourage him. He can be pretty damn persistent when it comes to women."

"I know," Simon said enthusiastically. "Go over to Halliday and tell him you just made a twenty-dollar bet with your friends that you could get him to kiss you. Tell him if he does it, you'll give him half."

"That's stupid," Frankie said scornfully.

"Actually, it's the best idea you've come up with so far." Leila pulled her eyes away from Marsh's quiet gaze.

"Then do it," Simon urged. "Come on. This music is starting to affect my central nervous system."

"It figures you don't like country music," Frankie sniffed.

"It figures you *do*," Simon said. He turned back to Leila and gave her a little push toward the bar. "Come on, Lei. Let's get this show on the road."

Marsh watched Leila slowly pick her way through the tables and chairs that dotted the floor. She was wearing a pair of khaki shorts that made her legs look long and graceful. She'd only been on the key for a few days, but already she had a decent tan. It was emphasized by the white tank top that hugged her upper body, outlining her slender curves. Leila wasn't a large-breasted woman. In fact she often found it unnecessary to wear a bra, a fact that Marsh was all too well aware of. But she wore one tonight, and one of the pale pink straps had slipped out onto her shoulder from beneath her shirt.

The woman looked positively delicious. With her cloud of golden curls, her beautiful eyes, her five-million-watt smile, and her friendly, funny disposition, Leila was going to enter Liam Halliday's field of vision and he was going to . . .

Marsh hurried across the room, after her.

"Leila, wait!"

He grabbed her arm, and her skin was soft and so smooth beneath his fingers. Startled, she spun to face him.

"Marsh, you scared me," she whispered.

"Sorry." He cleared his throat and wet his dry lips. "I'm sorry, I didn't mean to frighten you."

He was still holding her arm, and she didn't pull away, so he slid his fingers down to her hand and clasped her fingers within his.

"Look, Leila." He cleared his throat again.

She stood there, watching him silently, waiting for him to tell her . . . what? What was he going to tell her? That she didn't need to approach Liam Halliday because he, Marsh, was really the man she was looking for?

He almost said it. He cleared his throat yet one more time, but the words simply wouldn't come. He couldn't tell her. Not here. Not like this. "You don't have to do this."

Leila smiled. "I know that."

"You don't even know Liam Halliday," Marsh said quietly. "He's not perfect, in fact he's far from perfect. In quite a few ways, he'd be worse for you than your Elliot. He drinks way too much, for one thing. And he's known on the key to be something of a heartbreaker."

She smiled again, squeezing his hand very gently. "I can handle him."

Marsh smiled in return despite his trepidation. "You might think so. But Halliday's showing every sign of becoming an alcoholic. If I'm right about that, he's on a downward spiral that even you can't stop. He's got to stop it himself. But before he does, he'll take you down with him."

Leila frowned down at their entwined fingers. "I'm not going to marry the guy. I'm just going to have a conversation with him." She glanced up at him, her violet-blue eyes suddenly soft. "I'm glad that you care."

"I do," he murmured, his heart in his throat. This was it—the perfect time to tell her. Provided, of course, he could find the words. But, hell, he didn't have to use words. All he had to do was to lean forward and . . .

"He's gone," Frankie said flatly.

Marsh dropped Leila's hand and turned, startled, to see Frankie standing next to them, scowling.

"The sheriff just walked out the door," she informed them.

Marsh followed Leila's gaze as she looked over at the bar. Sure enough, Liam was gone. "Oh, no," she said.

"While you were standing here," Frankie continued, "Halliday got beeped, made a phone call, and left. Honestly, Leila, you've got to keep your mind on the job."

The next afternoon, Marsh found Leila out on the deck, tying the laces of her running shoes.

"You're back from work early."

He glanced ruefully at his watch. "Actually, it's nearly half four, and I'd hoped to be back before three. Look Leila, I'm in a bit of a bind. I just got a call from the Beauchamp boy. His parents aren't home. They drove over to the farmer's market on the mainland. It's going to take them at least three hours to drive back, and the family's mare has chosen this very moment to foal. I could use some help, mostly in calming Timothy down. He's only ten years old. He has this rather inconvenient habit of fainting from excitement and—"

Leila stood up. "I'd be glad to help. Let's go."

Her red running shorts were very, very short, and her skintight black top ended just below her breasts, exposing a wide expanse of her flat, tanned stomach. She looked slender and athletic and Marsh wanted desperately to touch her, to run his fingers over all that wonderful, smooth skin. He smiled at her instead, then turned, leading the way out to the driveway.

"This is probably unnecessary," Marsh said as they climbed into the jeep. He started the engine with a roar and left the driveway before Leila even got her seat belt fastened. "Timothy has the tendency to be overly melodramatic. Even though he seemed so convinced that something is wrong, that the mare is in trouble, I'm sure everything's all right—I'll probably just stand by and let nature take its course."

Yesterday, Marsh had driven her brother's jeep the same way he used to drive his little convertible sports car—nice and easy, with one hand on the steering wheel and the other resting casually on the gear shift. But today, both hands gripped the wheel, and he was driving at least fifteen miles per hour faster than the speed limit.

"Still," Marsh continued, "this mare is a major source of income for this family. If something were to happen to it, the Beauchamps would be in even worse shape financially."

Leila watched him as he drove. He looked incredibly handsome this afternoon—almost as good as he had looked last night at the Rustler's Hideout. He was wearing a crisp, new pair of navy slacks and a clean white shirt, nothing worn or secondhand today. In the backseat of the jeep, she could see a nice sports jacket and a tie. Whatever he'd been doing earlier that afternoon, he'd been wearing his very best clothes to do it. "You look nice. What's the occasion?"

He glanced at her. "I had a meeting with the building inspector."

"The building inspector?" Leila said. "Why?"

Marsh shifted into a higher gear, making the tires of the jeep hum as they sped even faster along the road. "I have to decide what I'm going to do about the house. If I don't start rebuilding soon, they're going to condemn the place." The muscles worked in his jaw as he stared otherwise expressionlessly at the road. "And they're right. As it stands, the house *is* a health hazard."

He glanced over to find Leila watching him. He hadn't fooled her. He could see in her eyes that she knew how upset he was.

"Did they give a date, a deadline? How soon are they talking about?"

Marsh shook his head. "I don't know. I don't care. I've got Timothy Beauchamp to worry about right now."

He didn't care about the deadline? That wasn't remotely true. But it was clear to Leila that he didn't want to talk about his financial problems right now.

"Don't forget about the horse," she said lightly. "She's the one in labor."

Marsh glanced at her again in surprise. She'd let him change the subject. "Somehow I think Tim probably is the more frightened of the pair."

"Back when you were at Harvard Medical School, did you ever even dream that someday some of the babies you'd deliver would have four legs and a tail?"

She wasn't pressing him about his financial woes. That was strange. He'd expected her to question him relentlessly until he spilled all of the vital information.

And it wasn't as if she simply didn't want to know. She did. He could tell that she was curious. But for some reason, she'd backed off. She'd given him space instead of the third degree. It was thoughtful of her, and sweet.

Impulsively, he reached over and took her hand. "Thank you."

"What, for asking you a silly question?" she said with a laugh.

"Yes." Marsh gave her hand a gentle squeeze before he released it. "Exactly for that."

"One of these days you're going to get out your accounts books and we're going to sit down and figure out a financial plan. And it better be soon. You're running out of time in more ways than one. I'm leaving in a little more than a week."

Marsh nodded. That was a fact he was all too aware of. Nine days and Leila would be getting on a plane, heading back north to New York City. "How about tonight?" he asked.

"Great. After dinner we lock ourselves in Simon's den."

The image of the two of them on the soft leather sofa in Simon's home office was tantalizing . . . and frustrating. He and Leila would be talking business, not making love. But, oh, it didn't take much imagining to picture her in his arms, kissing him the way she'd kissed him at Simon's party, molding her lithe body against his and . . .

Marsh hit the brakes hard, nearly missing the turn to the Beauchamp's farm.

Nine days and she'd be gone.

But not if he could bloody well help it.

SIX

From the moment Marsh stepped into the barn, he knew that the Beauchamp's mare was in serious trouble. Bright red blood smeared the inside of the stall and matted the straw that covered the hard dirt floor. The horse stood unsteadily, head down and eyes glazed.

Timothy was there, waiting for them. His face was pale and streaked with tears, but his mouth was set in a grim line of determination. "I know she should be lying down, but when she did, she started to roll, and I knew that would hurt the foal, so I've kept her up and walking."

"Splendid," Marsh said crisply, unbuttoning his shirt. "First thing *I* need to do is wash up and change. Tim, there's a packet of sterile green medical scrubs and gloves in the back of the jeep. Run quickly and get it. Leila, love, help me out of these clothes."

Leila couldn't move. Did he just ask her to help him take off his clothes? He couldn't possibly be serious.

"Get these shoes off, will you please?" Marsh asked. "Come on, quickly now."

Leila forced herself to kneel on the barn's packed dirt floor. She pulled off Marsh's dark brown dress shoes as he balanced first on one foot and then the other. He fumbled with the last of the buttons on his shirt, and finally yanked it over his head, tossing it over a wooden chair.

He was serious. He was actually taking off his clothes. Right there. Right in the barn. Right in front of her. And he wanted her to help.

But of course. His new clothes would be ruined if he went into the stall to help the mare. Still, it was extremely strange.

"Get the buckle, would you?"

Marsh had a white T-shirt on underneath his dress shirt, and as he pulled that off, Leila unbuckled his belt. As she started to unbutton his pants, his hands closed around hers.

"I'll get that."

Their eyes met for a fraction of a second, and Leila felt herself blush. What was she doing, reaching for his pants as if she couldn't wait to see the color of his shorts? And now he was smiling at her discomfort, the creep.

"You *asked* me to help," she said defensively, as he peeled his pants off his legs.

White. He was wearing plain, white, utilitarian briefs. They hugged his muscular body, contrasting with his tanned skin. Somehow she'd always pictured Marsh wearing expensive silk boxers.

Was he going to strip down even further? Leila held her breath, not knowing what to expect, hoping . . . what? That he would or that he wouldn't? She wasn't quite sure.

"I did ask you to help, indeed." Marsh crossed to the big sink in the corner of the barn. "But I thought it best to keep the distractions down to a minimum. I'm here to help the Beauchamps' mare, not live out one of my wildest dreams. Do me a favor, Lei, and take my socks off while I wash up? If I'm going to go shoeless, I'd much rather have bare feet."

Just then, Tim ran in, breathless, tears threatening. "I'm sorry, Doc, I can't find it."

Marsh looked up. "In the bag, Tim. In the bag in the back of the jeep." He smiled. "Take a deep breath and calm down. Everything's going to be just fine."

Tim nodded and scurried off.

Marsh turned on the hot water and began to scrub his hands and his arms all the way up past his elbows as Leila knelt down behind him. He balanced on one foot as she lifted his other leg. Her fingers felt cool against his skin, and her touch was gentle. It wasn't hard at all to imagine her hands caressing him. God knew, he'd imagined it often enough before.

Horse, Marsh thought almost desperately. He had to keep his mind on the horse. He was standing there in his underwear, after all. And his tight-fitting briefs didn't leave much to the imagination. But how many times had he fantasized about Leila? How many times had he dreamed of her taking off his clothes? Of course, he'd never included a mare in labor and a worried little boy in those dreams.

"Wildest dreams," Leila mused. "Right. By that I assume you're talking about this wonderful opportunity you have to embarrass me."

"Embarrass *you*," Marsh repeated in disbelief, rinsing the soap from his arms and hands. "Get the water, will you please?"

Leila reached over and shut off the faucet. "Yes. Embarrass *me*."

"But *I'm* the one standing here, definitely under-dressed for this particular occasion," Marsh said. He held up his hands so the water dripped down to his elbows. "*I'm* the one who's embarrassed."

It was so typical of Marsh. He was standing there with his nearly perfectly sculpted body, looking better than a man had a right to, looking as if he could start a new career modeling men's underwear if he ever tired of medicine. Yet, knowing Marsh, he'd probably never looked into a mirror. He probably had no idea how in-credibly delicious-looking he was. All he probably knew was that it was awfully improper to hang out in a barn in his underwear while accompanied by his best friend's sister. Leila had to laugh.

"Perfect." He closed his eyes briefly. "Most excel-lently perfect." He looked at Leila through the hair that had fallen into his eyes. "I'm nearly naked, the mare is in obvious trouble, and young Tim has turned an everyday errand into the search for the Holy Grail. All right, go on. Laugh at me. Get it all out of your system, then."

He *was* embarrassed. There was a tinge of pink

across his cheeks. He turned his back on her, crossing the barn to look into the mare's stall. "After you're done laughing," he added tightly, "trot on out and see what's keeping Tim."

He actually thought she was laughing at him. "Marshall, you colossal idiot." Leila rolled her eyes. "I'm not laughing at you. I mean, I *am* laughing at you, but not at the way you look. At the risk of inadvertently giving you a compliment, I've got to tell you that there are few men who look as good in their underwear."

He faced her with an overdone sigh of weariness. "Just go get Tim."

"You don't believe me. I can't believe you don't believe me—"

"I do," he said, clearly humoring her. "I believe you. I believe everything you say. Now, get Tim."

Timothy burst back into the barn, waving the plastic-wrapped packet that contained Marsh's scrubs and gloves. "This it?" he called.

"That's it. Good boy. Give it to Leila."

Leila glared at him as she took the packet from Tim and pulled out a pale green V-necked shirt and a pair of green pants. It was maddening when Marsh patronized her like this.

"Help me on with it, will you, please?" Marsh asked her. "My hands are clean."

Help him get dressed. Yes, that was a good idea. She could stand to have him look less like a Chippendale dancer and more like a medical doctor.

Still, helping him get dressed meant she'd have to stand really close to him and breathe in his clean, masculine scent, and feel the heat that was rising from his body.

But she was annoyed with him, Leila reminded herself. They were arguing, as usual. As long as they were arguing, she wouldn't have to worry about doing something foolish, like running the palms of her hands across the smooth expanse of his shoulders or . . .

"Is it possible for you, at least *once* in your life, to talk to me without being pompous and condescending?" she asked almost desperately as she yanked the shirt over Marsh's head. The backs of her knuckles ran all the way down the washboard muscles of his chest and stomach as she pulled the shirt down. She prayed that he wouldn't notice how hard it was for her to breathe, and she clung to their argument as if it were a lifeline. "Is it possible for you to speak to me as if I weren't some awful, spoiled child?"

The pants. Dear God, now she had to help him on with the green drawstring-waisted pants. Leila's mouth went dry as she knelt down in front of him and gazed at his strong legs.

"Funny you should mention that," Marsh retorted as Leila held one of the pants legs open for him to step into. He touched her bare shoulder lightly to keep his balance, and Leila nearly fell over. "Because I was wondering if it was possible for you, at least once in *your* life, to stop acting like a spoiled child."

Ooh, that comment stung, and for half a second, Leila forgot to feel flustered at pulling the pants up Marsh's muscular thighs and over his perfect rear end.

"You just hate it when I'm right," she said. "And I'm always right, which drives you crazy."

She adjusted the waistband of the pants, her hands up underneath the oversized scrub shirt, her thumbs running along his waist, from back to front.

"You definitely drive me crazy." Marsh's voice sounded oddly hoarse.

Leila glanced up into his eyes, then quickly looked away, concentrating on tying the cloth drawstring around his waist. Dear God, was it possible that he was affected by their nearness, too?

"You have absolutely no idea to the extent of how utterly crazy you drive me," Marsh continued. "And it has nothing to do, whatsoever, with your being right, since you spend so much time being wrong."

Leila glared up at him, gasping at his words.

"It also has nothing to do with your nasty habit of exaggeration," Marsh added. "Gloves, please."

He held up first one hand and then the other as Leila helped him on with a pair of surgical gloves. They were nearly impossible to put on, adding the final touch of frustration to this entire bizarre experience.

"You drive *me* crazy when your hair is in your eyes. Which it *always* is, and that's *not* an exaggeration," Leila practically exploded. With one hand, she raked his hair back, out of his face.

He turned his head so her hand brushed against the late afternoon stubble of beard on his chin. Before she could pull her hand away, he kissed the inside of her wrist, dragging his lips up to the palm of her hand.

Get 4 *Loveswept*® Romances FREE!

Get 4 Loveswept Romances FREE!

No Risk. No obligation to purchase. No commitment.

Leila felt nearly burned, and she quickly snatched her hand back. My God, he'd *kissed* her.

"I wear my hair this way," Marsh said, pushing open the door to the mare's stall with his elbow, "because I love driving you crazy."

He smiled at her, a triumphant, victorious grin.

Leila scowled, trying to hide the flush that she felt heating her cheeks. He'd *kissed* her. "Is it possible for you, at least once in your life, *not* to act like a jerk?"

"Shhh." Marsh carefully approached the mare. "Only positive energy, please."

He spoke softly and soothingly as he moved from the mare's head to her flank. Continuing to murmur quiet words, he crouched down and examined the horse.

Leila watched Marsh's face, and she knew from the sudden tightness of his mouth that the situation was not good.

Then, without warning, the mare kicked. Her hoof connected with Marsh's right shoulder with a solid thud, and the force was enough to push him backward. He hit the far wall of the stall with a muffled curse and went down onto the dirt floor.

"Marsh!" Leila was next to him in a flash. She pushed his hair back, out of his face, more gently this time.

Leila's hands against his forehead felt so cool, so soothing. And the anxiety in her eyes was more gratifying than he would have believed possible. She cared, that much was clear. But this was not the time to see whether her concern was that of one human for another, or something more. He was going to have to work quickly if he was going to save the mare's life.

Marsh pushed himself up into a sitting position, wincing as he first touched his shoulder, then rotated his arm. "Excellent. Glad to see the mare's still got quite a bit of strength left."

"Are you all right?" Leila demanded.

"Just bruised. No big deal. I'll live." He looked ruefully down at his gloved hands, now covered with muck and straw. "So much for being sanitary. Help me pull these off. Please?"

Leila's worry melted into anger. He could see it in the tension in her shoulders, in the set of her mouth, in the way her eyes seemed to flash.

"No big deal," she repeated his words as she peeled the gloves off his hands. "If that horse had aimed a little higher, or if you'd been leaning down a little lower, you would've been kicked in the head. You know, Dr. Smartass, people have been killed from being kicked in the head by a horse."

"But I was kicked in the shoulder," Marsh pointed out. "Not in the head."

He could very well have been badly hurt. She could've been sitting there, right now, with the island's only medical doctor dying in her arms of a head injury. What would Marsh do, she wondered with horror, if he ever actually *did* get hurt? Who would take care of him? Who would have the knowledge to save his life?

"You weren't kicked in the head . . . *this* time."

Marsh pulled himself to his feet. Leila could see that he was favoring his right shoulder even though he was trying to hide it from her. "Is this particular argument going to take very long? Because I don't have time for it right now."

"You'll have plenty of time," Leila shot back, her voice trembling with emotion. "An eternity, in fact, after this horse's foot connects with your skull and permanently scrambles the few brains you have."

"Your point is taken." Marsh looked back at the mare. "Love, do me a favor—"

Leila laughed. Her eyes were bright with tears, Marsh realized.

"What, help you get yourself killed?" She shook her head, her blond curls bouncing in emphasis. "No, thank you."

"Fine, then do Tim a favor and take him back up to the house." He stepped closer to Leila and spoke swiftly and softly so only she could hear him. "The foal's already dead, has been for quite some time. He's tangled in the umbilical cord and twisted around backward. I can save the mare, but it's not going to be a pretty sight."

They'd arrived too late. Leila could see compassion and regret in the warmth of Marsh's eyes. Strange, she'd always thought of him as emotionless, but now, when she looked closely, rarely a moment passed when she didn't see *something* stirring in his eyes.

"I'm sorry." She encircled Marsh's waist with her arms and held him tightly. She closed her eyes, burying her face in the warmth of his shoulder. "Be careful. You better be careful."

She felt him nod. "I will," he whispered.

It was unreal. Leila—lovely, vibrant, amazing Leila—

was in his arms again, but he couldn't kiss her. Not with young Tim looking on. Not with the mare's life hanging in the balance. Damn his poor timing anyway.

Leila lifted her head. Marsh's hair was in his eyes again, so she pushed it off his face one last time, running her fingers down the back of his head to his neck. Briefly she squeezed his shoulder. "Promise?"

The touch of her hand conveyed the warmth and strength of her feelings for him—feelings of friendship. Marsh turned away, suddenly and painfully aware that her earlier concern had been that of a friend, not a lover.

"Absolutely," he managed.

Dear Lord, he was in love with a woman who saw him as nothing more than an unrelated sibling, someone to squabble and argue with, someone to offer care and support to in times of need.

"Go on. Get Tim out of here."

He saw Leila as his hope, his future. It was true, the idea of a lasting relationship scared him to death, but without her, he knew that there'd be nothing but emptiness in his life.

Yet she saw him only as a brother.

Splendid.

Perhaps he *needed* a good swift kick in the head.

Marsh was quiet as he drove the jeep down the Beauchamps' dirt driveway.

"You did a good job," Leila said.

"Hmm." Marsh's eyes didn't leave the pitted road.

The jeep's headlights bounced as the wheels hit a pothole he couldn't avoid.

"You told me yourself there was no way you could have helped that foal, that he'd died before his mother even went into labor. And Kevin Beauchamp sure seemed grateful that you managed to save the mare."

Timothy's parents had arrived from the mainland as Marsh was cleaning up in the barn.

"Kevin was counting on the money from the future sale of that foal." Marsh pulled out onto the main road. "I don't know what he's going to do now."

"Speaking of money." Leila turned toward him.

He glanced warily at her, his face lit by the light from the dashboard.

"How can Kevin Beauchamp afford to pay you?"

"Ah, thank God," Marsh said. "I was afraid you were going to ask a more difficult question."

"I'll bet Kevin considers this one a pretty difficult question." Leila watched him steadily.

Her blond hair seemed almost unearthly in the darkness, gleaming in the light from the oncoming headlights. Marsh could still remember exactly how soft her hair had felt against his chin when she put her arms around him. The ache of longing that memory set off caught him by surprise. It stabbed him in the chest, sharp and hot. It took him a few seconds before he regained his breath.

"Actually," he replied, trying hard to make his voice calm and even, "it's a simple question because it's got a simple answer. He can't afford to pay me."

"Can't."

Marsh glanced at Leila again. She didn't seem surprised or even upset. Just resigned.

With no other cars approaching them, he could barely see her face in the soft glow from the dashboard. She looked mysterious and tantalizingly exotic. That fierce longing came back and he clenched his teeth, trying to fight it.

He didn't even know what this feeling meant, dammit. Well, okay, he knew what part of it meant. Part of it was sexual. He wanted her. There was no doubt about that. He'd wanted to make love to Leila since the summer she turned eighteen. Before that even, God help him. But there was more to this intense longing than sex.

Possession. He felt possessive. He wanted to own this woman in a very basic, almost primitive way—although, good grief, he could just imagine Leila's cries of outrage if he ever, ever tried to articulate that feeling.

Protection. He wanted to take care of her. He wanted to hold her close after their passion subsided and surround her with the warmth of his love.

Perfection. He wanted to feel forever this odd sensation he felt when Leila smiled into his eyes. It was more than happiness and bigger than mere satisfaction. It was the feeling that finally, *finally* he was completely whole. And he wanted to wake up every morning whistling because he knew that Leila would be smiling at him today. Today and tomorrow and the next day and the next.

"So he'll just never pay you?" Leila asked. "You'll just swallow the expenses of the medical supplies you used tonight, not to mention your time?"

"After they slaughter their hogs, the Beauchamps

will give me a year's supply of pork," Marsh explained. He couldn't look at her again . . . he didn't dare. This overpowering feeling just might run them both off the road. "In lieu of payment."

"Pork."

"And jam," Marsh added. "Kelly Beauchamp makes the tastiest raspberry jam I've ever—"

"You're a vegetarian," Leila said. "What could you possibly do with a year's supply of *pork?*"

"Well, obviously *I* don't eat it." He pushed his hair out of his eyes. He wished she'd just yell at him and get it over with. He could handle that better than this strange quietness. At least if she yelled, he'd know how to respond. At least that way he could measure her anger. "I give the pork to the Hopkins family. They live out on the point, about a mile past my house—I mean, where my house was."

"The Hopkinses. Have they lived on Sunrise Key long?" Leila asked.

"Since you were in high school. It's a big family. Five kids, all boys? They were quite a bit younger than you."

"I don't remember them," Leila admitted.

"They don't exactly run with the yacht club set," Marsh said dryly. "Ron's on disability right now, and with five teenagers, they could always use a year's supply of pork. Of course, it won't last them anywhere close to a year."

Leila was silent, looking at the darkness outside the jeep. "God, Marsh, I had no idea you were so . . ." She searched for the right word.

Marsh couldn't guess what she was going to say. So

stupid? So financially lame? So utterly, hopelessly in love with her?

"So incredibly perfect?" he suggested, pulling up to the stop sign at the intersection of Ocean Avenue and Main Street. "So dazzlingly handsome even when my clothes cover my underwear?"

She looked at him. In the dim light from the street-lamp on the corner, her eyes looked the purplish-gray color of the sky before a thunderstorm—dark and myste-rious with more than a hint of danger. It wouldn't take much to lose himself in those eyes. Marsh pulled his gaze away, only to find himself staring at her lips. God, but he wanted to kiss her.

"I had no idea you were so nice," she said.

It took a full three seconds for her words to register. *Nice?* Did she say *nice?*

Wait a minute, if she hadn't thought that he was nice before this, then what *had* she thought?

"I didn't realize you were so charitable."

"It's not charity," he said. If she didn't think that he was nice, then did she used to think that he was *not* nice? "Ron Hopkins would have a heart attack if he thought I was giving him charity. We trade. They have a huge garden. They keep me in zucchini and watermelon all season long."

"Most people wouldn't consider a year's supply of pork a fair trade for some measly fruit and vegetables."

"Most people aren't vegetarians, and therefore un-derrate the value of fruits and vegetables," Marsh pointed out. There was no traffic on either Main Street or Ocean Avenue. He put the jeep into neutral, and turned slightly to face her. "Look, Leila, if you had no idea that I was nice—"

"I had no idea you were so neighborly. What happened?"

"It must be contagious." Obviously she hadn't thought of him as friendly before this, either. "The people on the key look out for each other. You know how it works, you used to live here. The Hopkins kids weed old Mrs. Milton's garden. And Mrs. Milton always bakes an extra batch of cookies for the coffee hour after church on Sundays. Ben Sullivan uses his riding mower to cut the lawn in front of the town hall. Millie Waters always donates several cases of soda to the Little League to sell at their games."

"And you provide professional medical services for free."

"Not always for free. Some people have medical insurance. And others actually have money, believe it or not."

"Some doctors would refuse service to the people who couldn't pay."

"And some doctors will rot in hell," Marsh returned evenly. "I, for one, will go directly to heaven, through a special door marked Neighborly and Nice."

Leila laughed. God, he loved the sound of her laughter. He loved the way her smile seemed to include the entire universe. He loved the way her eyes seemed to dance with her amusement.

"You know, I honestly believe you will. Funny, I always thought . . ." Her smiled faded, and she looked away, as if she were embarrassed.

"Hmmm," Marsh said. A car drove up behind him, its headlights glaring in his rearview mirror. He reached out through the open side of the jeep and waved the driver past. "I suppose I better not press to find out the end of that sentence. It can't be anything good."

"I thought you were selfish and, well, self-centered," she admitted.

"And not very nice," he finished for her.

"I was wrong, wasn't I?" She looked back at him.

He could have answered her any number of ways. In fact, her statement begged to be picked up and returned to her sarcastically. According to her own words, she was never wrong, and admitting otherwise certainly deserved a caustic comment.

But Marsh didn't tease. He didn't joke. He didn't try in any way to mock her.

"I don't know," he said seriously. "There were times when I wasn't very nice to you. But only to you."

"Gee thanks. You know, when you and Simon were in college, you teased me mercilessly. You never let up. Half the time I was furious with you. The other half . . ." The other half of the time, she'd imagined herself almost in love with him. But there was no way she'd ever tell him that.

"You were always so rude to me," Marsh said. "Right from the first day I met you and Simon. You were what? Eleven years old? You were so blond and . . . American. You looked at me as if I were some worthless piece of garbage that had floated in on the tide. And you were just a child. Then when you got older, when you were in high school, you were *still* rude to me. Rude, and so bloody beautiful."

Leila stared at Marsh, but he was looking away from her, gazing out at the road ahead of them, as if he could see into the future.

"Beautiful? Right."

"You were. And still are."

Marshall Devlin thought that she was beautiful. Her heart was pounding so loudly, Leila was afraid he might be able to hear it. *Beautiful.* But . . .

She lifted one eyebrow. "So naturally you nicknamed me Monkey-Face?!"

Marsh looked at her and smiled. She could see his perfect white teeth, gleaming. "You don't seriously think I'd've given you the added ammunition of knowing that I thought you were the most gorgeous creature I'd ever seen in my life. Tell me honestly, wouldn't you have used it to tease me mercilessly in return?"

"Probably." She studied his face in the dim streetlight. "You really thought I was pretty? Back when I was in high school?"

"I remember one year you had a microscopic pair of cutoff blue jeans that were ripped up the side. They made your legs look even longer," Marsh mused. In the darkness his eyes looked dreamy—and *very* warm. "I spent the entire summer vacation in utter misery. You used to wear them with this little red-and-white halter top. You were so blond and tan. So perfectly American. Your smile—perfect. Your eyes—perfect. Your body— beyond perfect. I had a bloody heart attack every time you walked into the room."

"Oh, to be seventeen again," Leila said wistfully.

"You're twice as beautiful now."

Leila rolled her eyes. "And you're obviously twice as capable at slinging the b.s. I remember that my parents adored you. 'Why can't you be more like that nice Marshall Devlin?'" Leila mimicked her mother's voice. "'He's *so* polite.'" She shook her head. "You weren't polite, you were a liar."

Marsh shifted in his seat. "I believe the word you're looking for is *tactful*, not *liar*." He raked his hair out of his eyes. "Like most American teenagers, tact never was your strong suit."

"There's a difference between tact and kissing my parents' a—"

"Is *that* what you had against me?" Marsh interrupted. "Right from the start, you took an instant dislike to me. I remember the first time I came down to Sunrise Key with my father. It was Christmas, and I was miserable. If it wasn't for Simon . . . or maybe it was Simon. Was it because he and I became such good friends and you felt left out? Was that why you were so horrid?"

"Yeah, probably," Leila admitted. "At least partly. It was also because you were such a royal snob. You were so distant and, well . . . aloof. You never hung out with the other kids, only Simon. And I don't remember *ever* seeing you laugh. At least not that first year."

Another car's headlights appeared behind Marsh, and he waved it on. They'd been sitting there for a long time, Leila realized. But she was in no hurry to get home. She'd never talked to Marsh about any of this before—about all those ancient hurts and adolescent injustices that still lingered between them. She'd had absolutely no idea that he was attracted to her when she was a teenager. Why hadn't he ever asked her out? She would've said yes in a flash. Of course, he'd have had no way of knowing that.

"I didn't laugh very much, but surely even you could've given me the benefit of the doubt. I was seventeen years old, I was living in a new country with my father—whom I hardly knew—and his wife and their two children. I was suffering culture shock." He sighed. "And I was grieving."

Leila stared at him. "Grieving? Why?"

He stared back at her, leaning forward in the darkness. "You honestly don't know?"

"Marsh, what are you talking about?"

"My mother. She died, and one week later I was living in America, in a suburb of New Haven with this stranger who was my father. Two weeks after that, we were on vacation on Sunrise Key. I wasn't *aloof* when you first met me, Leila. I was numb."

"God, Marsh. No one ever told me." She covered her mouth with her hand, remembering all of the harsh words and dirty looks she'd sent in his direction as he'd stolen her beloved brother's attention. "I was so terrible to you. You must've thought I was an awful little bitch."

"I *did* think you were rather insensitive." He smiled ruefully. "And I must confess the word *bitch did* cross my mind a time or two."

"I'm sorry."

"I didn't realize you didn't know about my mother. I thought everyone knew." He laughed sadly. "It certainly explains quite a bit of your behavior. I always thought you had a rather cruel streak."

Leila closed her eyes and let her head fall back against the top of the seat. "I'm such a jerk."

"Leila, believe me, I've long since forgiven you."

Her exposed throat looked so long and slender in the light from the corner streetlamp.

"That doesn't make me less of a jerk."

"Past tense," Marsh pointed out. He had to clench his hands into fists to keep himself from touching her. "You *were* a jerk. You grew out of it. I grew out of a lot of things, too."

"Then why do I feel so awful?" She opened her eyes and turned her head to look up at him.

"Proof you're not a jerk. If you were a jerk, you wouldn't feel awful, right? It's in the past, Leila. Let it go."

"God, you *are* nice, aren't you? Sickeningly nice. I'm not sure I can stand it."

She was teasing him. She was teasing, because she didn't want him to see the sudden sheen of tears that had appeared in her eyes.

Marsh felt the bottom fall out of his stomach, as if he'd stepped off the edge of a cliff. Leila cared enough about him to cry. True, it was probably only a sisterly kind of caring, but that was certainly an improvement, considering as a teenager she'd apparently disliked him rather intensely.

Marsh did the only thing he could do. He pretended not to see the tears in her eyes. And he teased her back. "I suppose if you insist, I could start calling you

Monkey-Face again. I mean, simply to achieve a kind of balance in our relationship."

Leila laughed, and reached across the jeep to hug him.

This was it, Marsh realized. There was no way on earth he was going to be able to return Leila's embrace without kissing her. And when he kissed her, she'd know.

" 'Scuse me, folks," a voice said, and Marsh jumped. "Oh, hey, Doc. I didn't realize it was you."

Liam Halliday stood outside the jeep on Marsh's side, one hand on the edge of the vehicle's windshield, the other hand on the canvas top as he leaned over and looked in the open door. Marsh watched the tall sheriff take in every detail—Marsh's unbuttoned shirt, his jacket and tie and medical bag in the back, Leila's long arms and legs, her blond curls and pretty face.

"Ma'am." The sheriff nodded at Leila and touched his cowboy hat briefly. He smiled at her and reluctantly looked back at Marsh. "Havin' engine trouble, Doc? Can I help give you a push off the main drag here, and into the post office parking lot?"

The man's eyes kept returning to Leila. "Well, no." Marsh studied Halliday's face, trying to figure out what Leila saw when she looked at the sheriff. "Actually, the engine's fine. We were just having a chat."

Halliday had jet black hair that curled out from under the wide brim of his hat. One lock fell across his forehead, but it wasn't long enough to get into his eyes. Self-consciously, Marsh pushed his own brown hair off his face.

Halliday's eyes were brown, but darker than Marsh's. They were rich, deep, chocolate brown, while Marsh's were only the color of Tangled Neck Creek after a heavy rain, when the water was thick with mud and muck.

It was easy to overlook the fact that Halliday's eyes were bloodshot—no doubt from overindulging at the Rustler's Hideout the night before.

Leila reached across Marsh, holding out her hand for the sheriff to shake. "I'm Leila Hunt," she introduced herself with one of her more dazzling smiles. At least Halliday seemed dazzled, Marsh thought sourly.

"Liam Halliday," Halliday drawled, taking her hand and holding on to it much, much too long. "You related to Simon Hunt by any chance?"

"He's my brother."

"Have we met before?" Halliday asked. It wasn't a come-on, Marsh realized. There was honest puzzlement in the man's eyes. There were probably quite a few people a hard drinker like Halliday couldn't remember meeting.

"I'm not sure," Leila admitted.

Their clasped hands were inches away from Marsh's face, and he cleared his throat. Leila tugged her hand free.

"Well now." Halliday straightened up. "There's no parkin' so close to the corner, Doc." He grinned and winked at Marsh. "And particularly not in the middle of the road. I'm gonna have to ask you to move on. Or pull into the parkin' lot 'round the corner if you want to get friendly."

Leila blushed. "We were *talking*. That's all."

Marsh looked at her, eyebrow raised. She'd certainly been quick to make sure the sheriff knew there was nothing between them. Leila glanced at Marsh but quickly looked away, as if somehow he was the one who'd embarrassed her.

"Well, then, I beg your pardon," Halliday said. "Pull around the corner if you want to do some more . . . talkin'." He touched his hat and smiled at Leila again. "A pleasure meetin' you, Leila Hunt. See ya, Doc."

As Halliday sauntered back to where his police car was parked underneath the streetlight, Leila shook her head. "I can't believe Frankie won't go out with him. He's adorable."

"He's particularly adorable after he's spent the night in his own drunk tank," Marsh said dryly.

"Yeah, Frankie said he has the tendency to party." Her eyes followed Halliday. She watched as he reached into the front window of his car and pulled out the radio's microphone. "But she didn't tell me how amazingly good-looking he is. Ouch."

Ouch was right. "Yes, but does he look good while wearing only his underwear?" Marsh mused.

Leila laughed. "Probably not as good as you. Although . . ." Her eyes grew distant, dreamy. "Marsh, do you think he was the one?"

"No."

She looked at him in surprise. "How can you be so sure?"

"Do you really think Halliday might be your ninja?" Marsh countered. "I mean, *really?*"

She was watching the sheriff again. Was this jealousy

he was feeling? Yes, this was definitely jealousy, and it was far worse than the twinges he'd felt regarding Elliot. Elliot wasn't really a threat, despite Leila's talk of marrying the man. She might be thinking about marrying Elliot, but she clearly wasn't attracted to him, not like this.

Watching Leila gaze all starry-eyed at Halliday was dreadful. Marsh wanted to wring the sheriff's red neck, simply because the man existed.

"I honestly don't know. What if he *is* my ninja?"

"Well, what are you waiting for?" Marsh said, a touch nastily. "This is your big chance. Go and find out. Go and kiss him, why don't you? I'm sure he'll be more than happy to oblige." The way Halliday had been looking at Leila, it was more than clear that the man would be willing to let her run a series of test kisses on him.

Leila unbuckled her seat belt and slipped out of the jeep.

"Where are you going?" Marsh asked in surprise.

"You're right. This *is* my big chance. I'm going to talk to him. Pull into the post office parking lot. I'll be back in a few minutes, okay?"

"Leila, you can't be serious. *I* wasn't." But she was already walking toward the sheriff and didn't hear him.

He cursed under his breath as he watched them. The man already clearly thought that Leila was pretty. But there was so much more to her than her beautiful face and near-perfect body. She was smart and friendly and funny and warm. She was special. Even a damn fool like Liam Halliday would figure that out in a matter of seconds.

Halliday put away his radio microphone the second he spotted Leila walking toward him. He took off his cowboy hat and combed his fingers through his hair as he leaned against the side of his car. His long jeans-clad legs were crossed casually at the ankle.

Halliday smiled at Leila, and Leila smiled back, and Marsh knew that he couldn't, absolutely *couldn't* sit there and watch. He put the jeep into first gear and pulled around the corner into the parking lot in front of the post office. But, from where he parked, he could still see Leila and Halliday in his rearview mirror, so he closed his eyes.

Dammit, why didn't Leila smile at *him* that way?

Because she didn't see him as anything more than a friend, nothing more than another big brother. She'd been awfully bloody quick to correct Halliday when the sheriff assumed they'd stopped at the intersection to kiss. Was the idea of kissing him really that awful?

Leila certainly hadn't found him unappealing on New Year's Eve, when he'd kissed her at midnight. No, she'd responded to his kisses in a way that had nearly knocked him over.

Maybe that was the answer. Maybe he should dress up as the ninja and just appear in her room some night.

But, no.

The truth was, Marsh wanted Leila to love him. Not as a friend, not as a brother, not as a romantic phantom. He wanted her to fall desperately, hopelessly, tragically in love with him. With *him*, not some mysterious ninja.

And what, pray tell, were the odds of that happening?

Marsh opened his eyes, and in the rearview mirror, in the light from the streetlamp, he saw Liam Halliday draw Leila into his arms and kiss her. It was a long kiss, a slow kiss, a deep, passionate kiss.

Leaving the keys in the ignition, Marsh got out of the jeep and walked away.

SEVEN

"So you're standing there, in the middle of the road with the sheriff." Simon put his feet up on the top of the railing that surrounded the deck. "Then what? What did you say? 'Excuse me, Sheriff, would you mind giving me a kiss?'"

"Well, yeah." Leila stood across from him, looking out through the night toward the beach. The moon was out, and it was bright enough to see that the beach was deserted. No sign of Marsh.

Simon sat forward, pulling his legs back down. "You're not serious."

"Yes, I am. Simon, have you seen Marsh?"

"You told Halliday the whole story?"

"Not the *whole* story."

Simon pointed to a chair. "Sit," he ordered her. "I've *got* to hear this."

"I'm kind of in a hurry," Leila said. "Have you seen him?"

"Him who?"

"Marsh."

"Marsh?"

"Your friend? The doctor? Fairly tall, English accent, brown hair . . . ?"

Simon rested his elbows on his knees and his chin in one palm as he gazed up at her. "I know who he is. I'm just wondering why you're so hot to find him."

"We were supposed to go over his financial records." Leila finally sat down across from her brother.

"He's not here."

She gave him a piercing look. "Would he be here if I were looking for him for another reason?" she asked.

Simon laughed. "No. Believe me, I *want* you to help him organize his accounts. I tell you, Lei, for a guy with a medical degree from Harvard, Dev absolutely stinks at math. And it doesn't worry him. The man doesn't care." He shifted back in his seat. "So. Tell me about Halliday. What did you say, what did he say? I want details."

Leila closed her eyes. "I walked up to him and said, 'You know, I've been thinking. Maybe we *did* meet.' See, he'd asked me earlier if we'd met before. Then I asked him if he wore a ninja costume to your party, which of course I already knew."

"Brilliant move. Testing him to see if he was going to tell the truth or lie most heinously."

"No, you idiot," Leila said lightly. "He's the town sheriff. I didn't expect him to lie. I needed to have something to talk about, to break the ice, so to speak, so I asked him about his costume."

"Of course. You broke the ice. He said, yes, he was a ninja. Then what?"

"I told him I had been wearing a Cinderella costume, and I asked him if he happened to remember if I was the person he'd kissed at midnight."

Simon laughed, thoroughly enjoying himself. "I can't believe you actually had the nerve to ask him that. Go on. What'd he say?"

"Well . . ." Leila began. "This is where it got a little tricky. Apparently Liam wasn't a designated driver that night, and he'd had a little too much to drink—"

"His usual truckload of whiskey and beer," Simon interjected. "What else is new?"

"The end result being, much to poor Liam's embarrassment, that he doesn't remember exactly *what* he was doing at midnight. The evening all became one rather out-of-focus blur for him."

"He admitted that?"

"He did, although he spent about ten minutes trying to convince me—and himself, it seems—that this doesn't happen to him all the time. He said it was New Year's Eve and he let himself cut a little more loose than usual."

"Hmm," Simon said.

"Yeah."

"Then what?"

"Then we stood there for a few more minutes and both tried not to be embarrassed as he denied he has a drinking problem. He's never missed a day of work, he never touches the stuff when he's on duty, he only drinks to relax, blah, blah, blah. I heard it all. Every excuse in the book."

Leila took a deep breath, looking up at the moon and the stars in the inky blackness of the night sky. "So then," she continued, "when he stopped to take a breath, I interrupted him and told him about the man who had kissed me at midnight—who incidentally, certainly didn't *act* as if he were blind, stinking drunk."

"You *told* him? About the kiss?"

"Kisses. Plural. I gave him the G-rated version." Leila glanced ruefully in Simon's direction. "I told him I was looking for this man, that I wanted to find out who he was. I didn't go into detail as to why."

"Good thinking."

"Then I asked him if he would mind kissing me."

Simon nodded. "So what did you do when he said no?"

Leila tried to swat her brother on the top of the head with the palm of her hand.

"I was kidding." He ducked out of the way. "So he kissed you. Was he the guy you're looking for? Did you see fireworks, et cetera and so on?"

"No." Leila stared back at the stars. "No fireworks. Definitely not." She sighed. "And then, when I got back to the jeep, Marsh was gone."

Simon sat up. "*Marsh* was there? *With* you? While you were kissing Halliday?!"

Leila glanced over at him. "We were driving back from the Beauchamps'. I *thought* we were heading back here to have dinner and then go over Marsh's books. But he just disappeared. He left the keys in the jeep. I waited for a while, but he never came back. So I drove home. You're sure he's not here?"

"Oh, Leila. Oh, no." Simon buried his face in his hands. "No, he's not here. I should go look for him." He glanced at his watch. "But I've got a date in about fifteen minutes."

"Who's the unlucky woman?" Leila asked.

"You wound me," Simon said. "Her name's Amanda. She's the new waitress over at the Pier."

"Poor thing. Be gentle when you break her heart." Leila stood up. "If you see Marsh, tell him I'm looking for him. You can also tell him that one way or another, I *will* see his books. He's not going to get away from me this easily."

The sound of the telephone ringing woke Leila from a deep sleep.

" 'Lo?" she rasped into the phone, pushing her hair out of her eyes, and reaching over to turn on the bedside table lamp.

"Leila?"

"Yeah." She squinted at the clock in the sudden brightness. "Frankie? Is something wrong? It's two-thirty in the morning."

"You got *that* right," Frankie drawled. "I'm working the late shift for the cab company, and I got a call to pick up a customer over at the Rustler's Hideout, 'cause it's closing time. I got here a few minutes ago, and guess who that customer turned out to be?"

"Simon?"

"Good guess, but no cigar. You're on the right track though. Think a little thinner, a little shorter, brown hair instead of blond—"

"*Marshall?*"

"Bingo. Bartender says he's been here for hours. He doesn't really seem juiced, but he says he wants me to drive him home."

"Well, bring him on over." Leila swung her legs out of bed. "I'll put on a pot of coffee and—"

"*His* home," Frankie interrupted. "He wants me to drive him over to his burned-out house on the point, Leila."

Leila stood up, carrying the telephone with her as she went to her bureau and pulled out a pair of shorts, a T-shirt, and a clean pair of underwear.

"I wasn't sure what to do," Frankie continued as Leila pulled her nightie over her head and got dressed. "I mean, I can't drive him up there and just *leave* him. The house is wrecked. It's dangerous to go near it in broad daylight, let alone the middle of the night. And that's not even taking into consideration the man's blood-alcohol level. But he's insisting that's where he wants to go."

"I'll wake up Simon and we'll meet you up at the point. Drive slowly, though. It's going to take us a few minutes to get over there."

Frankie sighed with relief. "Thanks, Leila. Sorry I had to wake you."

"I'm glad you did." Leila hung up the phone and slipped her sneakers onto her feet.

Out in the hallway, the house was dark.

She walked softly down the hall toward Simon's room. His door was ajar, and she pushed it the rest of the way open. Moonlight streamed in through the windows onto his made-up bed.

Her brother wasn't home. And if she knew Simon, he probably wouldn't return for a while. Like not until sometime tomorrow afternoon.

She was going to have to do this alone.

Leila arrived at Marsh's house before the taxi. She pulled into the driveway and parked, then got out of the jeep to look at the ruins of the house in the moonlight.

It was in awful shape. Apparently, the house had burned for quite some time before anyone saw the smoke and sounded the fire alarm. The roof was gone, and three of the outer walls had caved in. The brick chimney stood alone, listing slightly to one side. It wouldn't take much more than a strong wind off the ocean to send the bricks tumbling down on top of the pile of ashes and charred lumber that used to be Marsh's house.

Strips of yellow police tape, printed with bold black letters, warned Danger, Keep Out! They'd been placed as a kind of barrier, encircling the ruined building. They had long since sagged and torn, and now flapped rather uselessly in the cool night breeze.

Leila heard the sound of a car engine and turned to see headlights approaching. She walked down the drive toward the taxi as it pulled up.

The inside light went on. Marsh was sitting in the

front seat. He gave Frankie the fare, then opened the door.

He clearly wasn't expecting to see Leila standing there. A wide range of emotions crossed his face, including pleasure and surprise before he settled on wariness.

"Well." He climbed carefully out of the taxi and closed the door behind him. "My word. This is a rather interesting surprise."

Frankie leaned across the front seat so she could see Leila. "I've got to run. I've got another fare to pick up. Must be the full moon. You gonna be all right?"

"Everything's under control," Leila said with far more confidence than she felt. In fact, the mere sight of Marsh—in particular that flash of uninhibited pleasure that had lit his eyes when he'd first spotted her—made her feel as if she were careening off the side of a mountain.

"Ah, I'm so glad to hear that," Marsh said. "I do hate it when things get out of control."

"You want me to swing past here later?" Frankie called.

"No, that's okay," Leila told her. "Go on. We'll be okay."

Marsh turned to watch the taxi slowly roll down the street, leaving them in the moonlight. The moon was nearly full, and so bright that it cast shadows around them.

Marsh still wore the white shirt and navy blue pants he'd changed back into at the Beauchamps'. At the time, his shirt had hung open, but now it was neatly buttoned and tucked into the waist of his pants.

He didn't look like a man who'd spent the past seven hours in a bar.

His hair was messy, but that was nothing new. His hair was nearly always messy. As he turned and caught Leila watching him, he self-consciously pushed it back, out of his eyes.

"So. You've come to rescue me, have you?"

Now that she could see his eyes, Leila wished that he hadn't pushed his hair back. He was watching her much too intently, hungrily even. In the moonlight, she could see heat in his eyes, heat from desire. Desire. He wasn't trying to hide it from her. In fact, she could have sworn that he stepped closer, tilting his head slightly, so that she would have a better chance to see it there in his eyes.

"That depends." Leila wet her suddenly dry lips. "Do you need rescuing?"

"More than you would believe."

Leila's pulse kicked up higher as she stared at him, trapped by the magnetic pull of his eyes. Oh, my God. Everything about him—the way he was standing, his body language, his smile, that unmistakable glint in his eyes—said "come and get me."

If she were eighteen again, she would've leapt at the chance to play this game with him. But she wasn't eighteen anymore. And games usually ended with a winner and a loser. One of them was bound to end up hurt, and it would probably be her. After all, she wasn't the one who'd spent the entire night drinking in order to lose his inhibitions.

Leila crossed her arms. "Oh, I'd believe you need

rescuing. While you were out, I took the opportunity to look at your financial records."

Marsh scratched his chin. "Funny, I thought I'd locked my bedroom door. Don't tell me you've taken up picking locks in your spare time."

"Our rooms are attached by a balcony," she reminded him. "And you didn't lock that door. It was wide open. So of course I went in."

"Of course," Marsh murmured.

"Your records are a mess. I'm not sure which is worse—your handwriting or your organizational skills."

"Rumor has it I'm a very good doctor." Marsh pushed himself up so that he was sitting on the hood of the jeep.

The heat in his eyes hadn't let up despite her attempt to discuss his least favorite subject—money. He'd purposely left space for her to sit next to him. He didn't pat the spot or gesture in any way, but his invitation couldn't have been more clear.

"That's one rumor I'd believe," she replied, moving several steps away from him. "I didn't realize that you'd specialized as a surgeon during your internship and residency. You gave up more than a high salary when you turned down that job in Boston, didn't you? You gave up an entire career."

Marsh finally looked away from her, lifting his chin to gaze up at the moon. The whitish blue light bathed his face, playing delicately over his high cheekbones and lean jawline, making his upturned eyes look oddly crystal clear and strikingly beautiful.

Leila stood, almost spellbound, just watching him.

She would have given just about anything to know what he was thinking.

And then, he spoke.

"Every choice you make in life, every decision you come to, means you're giving something up." He turned his head to look directly at her. "I gave up a chance of probably ever owning a Porsche. I gave up a career that probably would have made my name familiar to physicians all over the world. But what I gained is far more valuable. I gained a life that I'm happy with. I do a job that I'm proud of. Boston is just another city, another impersonal place where I have no ties, no roots." He shook his head. "I know you probably can't understand that. I don't know what I can tell you to make it any clearer. I know you don't feel the way I do about Sunrise Key. If you did, you wouldn't have left. But this island is my *home* now. I love it here."

Leila was astonished at Marsh's openness and the eloquence of his words.

"This island could be *your* home again, too," Marsh said softly. "You don't know what I'd give, Leila, to have you down here year-round."

Leila was staring at him as if he were speaking in a foreign language. God, she was beautiful in the moonlight. Her hair looked almost silvery instead of gold, and her skin seemed to glow.

A strong breeze occasionally gusted in from the Gulf, pressing her oversized T-shirt tightly against her slender curves, outlining her breasts in exquisite detail. She wasn't wearing a bra. She'd probably thrown her clothes on, assuming that he'd never know the difference.

She was wrong. Marsh always knew.

Her cutoff jeans were the same kind of shorts that had driven him nearly crazy back when she was a teenager. Had she worn them on purpose? No, from the way she kept backing off, it was clear that she hadn't come to seduce him.

But she *had* come.

What had Frankie told her? It had to be Frankie who called Leila. Did Frankie tell Leila that Marsh was at the Rustler's Hideout, sitting at the bar, drinking? And did Leila come because she thought that Marsh was half-seas over and unable to get home on his own?

The truth was, he'd had three gin and tonics all night. Six hours plus six ounces of gin did not add up to intoxication, despite the fact that he'd had his third drink right before the bar's last call. It was true that he wasn't a drinker. And it was also true that he nearly fell off his bar stool on the way to the men's room, but that was from light-headedness due to lack of dinner, not from the drinks. He was, quite honestly, only very slightly anesthetized. *Very* slightly.

Still, it was likely that Leila thought he was sozzled.

He opened his mouth to inform her otherwise, but then shut it again. Why tell her? This way he had the edge. This way he could say things he might not normally say. This way he could play the role, if need be.

"Look at this place," Marsh commanded her.

Leila turned and gazed at the ruins. "The house looks awful. God, Marsh, you're lucky you weren't inside—asleep. Can you imagine if—"

Shaking his head, he cut her off. "No, I didn't mean

the house. I meant the island—the ocean, the beach, the moonlight, the trees." He took in a deep breath through his nose. "Something's blooming. This is the time of year when the island is covered with flowers. It's gorgeous. It's *paradise*. How could you possibly have traded this for Manhattan?"

Leila sighed. "Marsh, I lived here for ten years."

"And you don't miss it? Not even a bit?"

She faced him. "Of course I miss it. But . . ."

"But what?"

The breeze blew again, and she hugged herself as if she were chilled. Marsh watched her stare sadly at the ruins of his house. "I was going to say that I love living in New York. But . . ."

Marsh waited, willing her to go on.

"But I don't know anymore," she said. "I see this road ahead of me, this future, and all I can feel is detached curiosity, as if it's someone else's life, not mine. I try to imagine myself spending the rest of my life with Elliot, living in the city, making all the right career moves, going through the motions. It should be so perfectly right, but to me it feels wrong. At the same time, giving it all up seems wrong, too."

"Maybe it's time to come home," Marsh murmured.

She turned to look at him and her eyes were so sad. "I spent every waking moment for nearly four years planning and scheming to get off Sunrise Key. Coming back here would feel like quitting."

"It's not—"

"I wish that I loved him." She took a deep breath and slowly exhaled. "But I don't."

She was talking about Elliot.

"Coming back to Sunrise Key *wouldn't* be quitting," Marsh said.

Leila shook her head. "Living here drove me nuts, Marsh. Everyone knows what everyone else is doing *all* the time. There's no privacy, no secrets, no surprises. I remember when my parents decided to start a vegetable garden. Doesn't seem like much of a topic for gossip, does it?" She laughed, and there were traces of despair in her voice. "But it was. I rode my bike down to the hardware store to pick up some chicken wire for fencing, and Mr. Lanigan had already set a roll aside for us . . . along with a tray of tomato seedlings, some wood stakes, and a garden trowel that had gone on sale."

Marsh leaned forward slightly. "But that's *nice*. If Mr. Lanigan hadn't set those things aside for you, they might've been sold to someone else."

"But I didn't tell him I was coming. My parents didn't tell him. He *assumed*, because someone had told him about our garden."

"Leila—"

"It was worse when I turned sixteen," she continued hotly. "I couldn't make a move without everyone in town knowing where I was and what I was doing there. Frankie and I tried to hitchhike off the island. Who picks us up? Sam Zimmer, the manager of my father's store." She rolled her eyes. "He drove us home and told us if he ever heard even the tiniest whisper of a rumor about us hitching again, he'd tell my father and I'd be grounded for the rest of my life." She snorted. "The big joke was, I was already grounded—I was stuck here on Sunrise Key."

Marsh realized he'd been holding his breath, and he exhaled swiftly. "Thank God for Sam Zimmer." He slid down off the jeep. "Can you imagine what might have happened if some off-islander had picked you up?"

"Of course," Leila said. "Now I know better, but—"

"I remember what you looked like when you were sixteen." Marsh ran his hand down his face. She'd looked like an angel, half child, half woman, pure temptation. "Christ, Leila, you could have wound up in a ditch. You might have disappeared, for good."

"I was a kid, Marsh. I needed freedom. I felt so suffocated and overprotected here." Another blast of chilly air came in from the water, and Leila shivered. "That's why I went to New York."

"So you could be raped and murdered whenever the mood struck?" Marsh asked, reaching into the back of the jeep for the sports jacket he'd left there earlier in the evening.

"Of course not."

"I can't *believe* you tried to hitchhike off the island. If I had known, I would have wrung your little neck!"

"Simon would have beat you to it." Leila sighed. "I can't come back here, Marsh."

"Yes, you can." Marsh opened his jacket. He'd intended to wrap it around Leila's shoulders, but she backed away, wary of his next move. Instead, he held it out to her. "You aren't sixteen anymore, Leila."

"Rub it in," she muttered, taking the jacket, careful

not to touch him. She slipped her arms into his jacket and closed the front.

"I'm serious." Marsh pushed himself back onto the jeep. "You have different needs now. What you saw as nosiness or lack of privacy when you were younger will turn into neighborliness, friendliness, concern, and caring . . . if you let it."

His jacket hid the bottom edge of her shorts, casting the illusion that she wore nothing underneath. It was a very nice illusion.

"You went to New York," Marsh continued, forcing his gaze away from her long, bare legs. "You tried it out. But I don't think the experiment worked. It sounds to me as if you don't like it there."

She didn't deny it. She just stood there staring at him with her luminous, beautiful violet-blue eyes.

"Don't go back," Marsh whispered. "You don't have to go back."

Leila turned away from the hypnotic warmth of Marsh's eyes. Her heart was pounding, and she was suddenly aware of her lack of oxygen. She laughed, because it covered her sense of unease. Was it possible that she was actually considering everything he'd said?

"What am I supposed to do?" she asked. "Fax all my clients, let 'em know my new address and phone number?" She met Marsh's gaze in the moonlight. "Send for all my things?"

"You could." His gaze was hot and piercingly relentless. "You could do it tomorrow. I'd help you, Leila. You can count on me for anything."

"Anything?" she repeated with a laugh. This whole

discussion was getting out of hand. "Watch out. You may not realize what you're offering."

"I'm offering everything," he said simply. He held out his hands, palms up. "Unconditionally."

Leila crossed her arms. "Oh, really?" She hoped he didn't hear the way his words made her heart beat faster and louder. He'd been drinking, she reminded herself. In the morning he probably wouldn't even remember what he'd said. "Then after I move down here and tell Elliot I'm not going to marry him, you'll volunteer to father my children?"

Marsh's eyes turned molten. "Father your children? Help with the fun part and leave you to do the rest?" He shook his head. "But don't misunderstand, love. It's not because I'm averse to the fun. On the contrary. That particular activity is one that I've longed—rather desperately, I might add—to do with you for years and years now."

Leila felt her face flush. He was talking about making love. He'd just admitted that he wanted desperately to make love to her. Any second now, he was going to slide off the jeep and walk over to her, and take her into his arms and . . .

And there was no one around to interrupt them. This time, he'd succeed. He'd kiss her and . . .

"It's not the idea of having children that doesn't appeal to me," Marsh continued. "I would like to have a few of my own. I just don't want them growing up without me."

He'd kiss her, and then, God help her, they'd probably end up making love right there on the lawn above the beach, out in the moonlight, under the stars.

Because that's what she wanted. She *wanted* to make love to Marsh Devlin.

And knowing that scared her to death.

Leila forced herself to turn away from the warmth in Marsh's eyes. "Your children wouldn't grow up without you." Her voice sounded unnaturally loud in the night's silence. "Considering that we'd all be living in the same place. If I moved back to Sunrise Key, we'd *all* be sponging off Simon, wouldn't we?"

She had, undoubtedly, succeeded in destroying the mood, in deflating the bubble of desire that had surrounded them both and drawn them closer and closer together.

Marsh slid off the jeep. "My word, I thought I was properly anesthetized and quite comfortably numb. Apparently I was wrong. It seems to have worn off. Or perhaps that barb had a particularly sharp point." He pushed his hair back from his face and stood for a moment, staring at the ruins of his house. "I don't suppose you brought along anything potent to drink?"

"No."

"No, of course you didn't. Pity. God, this place is a mess, isn't it?"

Leila felt awful. She hadn't meant for her comment to be quite that cruel. "Marsh, I'm sorry, I—"

"I changed the subject, Leila," he said quietly, not meeting her eyes. "That conversation was apparently going nowhere. Let's move on, shall we? I came out here to have a look at the house, try to decide what to do."

His face was shadowy in the moonlight. "See, I gave the building inspector a call tonight. I told him to tear the place down, get the mess cleaned up. Now what I need to decide is whether or not to leave the foundation intact. Whether to rebuild or sell."

"Sell?"

"Believe it or not, there's actually something you *don't* know." He turned to look at her. "I received an offer for this land . . . an offer well above market value."

"From Preston Seaholm." Leila pulled Marsh's jacket tighter around her shoulders as another cool breeze blew in from the Gulf. "I *do* know about it. There was a letter from him in your room."

"So much for privacy," Marsh muttered. "For someone who cares so much about it, you certainly don't honor it, do you? I suppose you went through my underwear drawer while you were at it."

"The letter was stuffed into a file marked Received," Leila said indignantly. "It was among a pile of insurance checks . . . that you haven't cashed, I might add."

"You always do have something to add, don't you? So what's your advice? Let's hear it, Leila. Should I sell or not?"

She felt like crying. All of the warmth in Marsh's eyes was gone. He leaned back against the jeep and gazed at her with that mocking glint that was part amusement and part disdain.

"I think it would be wise to sell, particularly for what he's offering."

"His offer is really little more than charity," Marsh

said flatly. "It's Seaholm's way of helping me out of this financial bind."

"He *does* get the land."

"The same way I get watermelon and zucchini when I trade the Hopkinses for all that pork."

"Pres Seaholm has a vested interest in keeping you here, on the key," Leila pointed out. "You're the only doctor in more than forty miles. Besides, if that kind of trading doesn't bother the Hopkinses, why should it bother you? You said it yourself. That's just the way things work down here. People look after each other. Is it so terrible if someone does a little looking after you?"

"You didn't like it when people looked out for you." Marsh stared at the burned shell that was once his house, his home. "I like this particular view of the ocean. I don't want to sell." He looked at Leila. "I've decided. I'm going to rebuild." He smiled. "There. That was easy, wasn't it?"

"Even with those insurance checks I found, you're still forty-four thousand dollars short," Leila warned him. "But if you want, I can help you organize your financial records. You'll stand a better shot at getting a bank loan and—"

"I can rebuild without borrowing any money from the bank," Marsh said.

"What, you're planning to win the lottery?" Leila crossed her arms.

"Sort of." Marsh went around to the passenger side of the jeep. "Drive me back to Simon's. It's time for me to sponge off the bastard a bit more."

Leila sighed with exasperation. "Marsh, I don't know why I said that."

"Forget about it." He climbed into the jeep. "Come on, the sooner we get back, the less hellish I'll feel in the morning."

But she *did* know why she'd said such a cruel thing to Marsh.

She had been terrified.

Marsh had been talking about making love to her. He'd as much as confessed that he wanted her, desperately. That word still echoed in her head. *Desperately. Desperately . . .*

And Leila wanted him, too. She wanted him to make love to her. She wanted it badly, desperately. Desperately . . . Forget about the ninja. Forget about Elliot. Forget about her job as an accountant back in New York City. Forget about everything but Marsh and the way he could make her heart pound with just a look and a smile.

It was terrible, it was awful, but it was undeniable.

Leila had it bad for Marshall Devlin.

EIGHT

The lifeguard chair stood like a sentinel on the white sandy expanse of the town beach. The afternoon was hot and still, and Hayden Young, the lifeguard, opened the colorful beach umbrella that was attached to the back of his chair.

Leila and Frankie sat in their beach chairs and tried not to stare, at least not too obviously.

Hayden was everything Frankie had said he was. Blond, tanned, and muscular. As she strolled casually past the lifeguard chair, Leila had even had a glimpse of the electric blue eyes he normally kept carefully hidden behind a pair of sunglasses.

He was almost laughably gorgeous.

His hair was long and thick, and he wore it back in a ponytail. His jaw was strong, his cheekbones were chiseled, and his nose was perfect, just the right size for his face.

"So this is what's coming out of the university's philosophy program these days," Leila mused, spreading more sunblock on the tops of her feet and that one badly sunburned place she had along the edge of her bathing suit. Lord, it was hot today. She wished *she* had an umbrella to shade herself, too.

"He's also a trained EMT," Frankie reminded her. "You know, he's teaching a CPR course down in the church basement over the next four Monday nights. I tried to sign up. I figured in my line of work, CPR might be good to know. But apparently, the class was filled to capacity weeks ago."

Leila grinned. "You could always ask him for private lessons."

"Or *you* could. You're the one who wants to kiss him."

They watched as several little children approached the lifeguard chair carrying a yellow bucket. They talked to Hayden, craning their necks, pointing inside the bucket. Hayden climbed down from his perch and crouched in the sand to talk to the children.

"My God, he's nice to kids, too," Leila said, "Tell me, honestly, what would you do with a guy who's that good-looking? Everywhere you went, you'd have a swarm of women following. Or at least looking."

"And drooling," Frankie added. "Definitely drooling. It would get very soggy."

"Who needs it?" Leila asked. "Not me."

"Me neither."

Hayden Young ruffled one of the boys' hair and waved good-bye as the children ran off. He climbed up the ladder to his chair, his muscles rippling in the sunshine.

"On the other hand . . ." Frankie said.

"Mmm, I know what you mean."

They lapsed into silence, and Leila closed her eyes. Her ninja hadn't been Liam Halliday or Preston Seaholm. Hayden Young was last on her list of suspects, except for good old married Robert Earle in Atlanta. But what if it hadn't been Earle either? That would mean that somewhere on Sunrise Key there was another ninja.

But who could it be?

Leila tried to remember the night of Simon's party, tried to remember the man who had silently asked her to dance, who hadn't taken no for an answer.

Hayden Young's shoulders were awfully broad. Had her ninja really had shoulders like that?

Try as she might, she couldn't conjure up any clear memory of her mystery man. Except for those kisses. If he kissed her again, she'd recognize him, that was for sure. But as far as his height and weight and the width of his shoulders went, she couldn't remember a thing.

Instead, a picture of Marsh, sitting on the hood of the jeep, gazing at her in the moonlight, kept popping into her head.

He'd left the house before she even woke up this morning. Simon told her that Marsh had scheduled appointments all day; he wouldn't be back until nearly seven o'clock.

Marsh must feel like hell. He wasn't a heavy drinker, in fact he barely ever touched the stuff. He'd told her years before that he stopped drinking after he went to medical school and found out exactly what alcohol did to the human body. He'd become a vegetarian at about the same time.

"What's your plan for Hayden Young?" Frankie asked. "Are you gonna go for the direct approach again? The way you did with the sheriff?"

"I don't know. Hey, Frankie?"

"Yeah?"

"What do you think of Marsh Devlin?" She opened her eyes and looked at her friend.

Frankie was wearing sunglasses, so Leila couldn't see her eyes, but her eyebrows were definitely raised.

"The accent's to die for, and he's really good-looking. Different from the beach boy," she added, gesturing toward Hayden with her chin, "but still handsome." She shrugged. "He's got nice hands, too. Remember the time I thought I broke my ankle? Marsh checked it out. It hurt like hell, but it would've been a lot worse if he hadn't been so gentle. He seems nice. He's always so polite. . . ."

Leila sat forward, "But?"

"He's so reserved." Frankie smiled apologetically "I don't know, Lei, it's hard for me to be objective because he's definitely not my type of guy." She grinned. "Of course, I haven't quite figured out yet who my type of guy is. But Marsh, he's too chilly, you know? Like if you get too close, you might freeze to death."

Leila shook her head. "I used to think that, too. But lately, when I'm around him I definitely don't feel as if I'm going to freeze to death."

"Using my superior observational skills as a private

detective, I'd say you sound like you'd rather kiss Marsh Devlin than Hayden Young."

"Isn't that weird?" Leila said. "Marsh and I have done nothing but fight for years, and now, all of a sudden, I feel as if there's some bizarre magnet pulling me toward him. I've been really talking with him, too. I've been finding out things about him that I never knew before. He's not at all chilly, not even close. He's warm and kind and wonderfully sweet . . . and I sound like an idiot, don't I?"

Frankie grinned. "Do you remember that summer back in high school when you had a crush on Alan Johnson?"

Leila shook her head. "This isn't a crush."

"I know," Frankie said. "Back *then* you sounded like an idiot, going on and on for hours about how Alan wore his hair and the shape of his chin, and whether or not his hitting his car horn whenever he drove past you on Main Street meant something. What you're saying now sounds very different to me."

Leila closed her eyes and lifted her face to the warm sunshine. It sounded different because it was different. What she felt about Marsh wasn't a schoolgirl crush. It was more than that. It was bigger. It was . . . No, she couldn't even bring herself to *think* the *L*-word.

Falling in love wasn't a bad idea. In fact, it was something she'd always hoped would happen to her. But falling in love with Marshall Devlin was the last thing she wanted to do.

Marsh wanted her to move back to Sunrise Key, to be reabsorbed by the small-town life that she'd worked so hard to leave behind. But she prided herself on her independence. If she came back, she'd be treated like a child again. She'd suffocate from the lack of privacy.

Yet . . .

Leila opened her eyes and glanced over at her friend. Frankie wasn't suffocating. Frankie had lived on Sunrise Key all her life, but she didn't feel penned in or trapped by the constant gossiping and prevalent nosiness. In fact, she joined in, happily keeping track of the island's goings-on.

But they were two different people, with two different sets of priorities.

Leila sighed, closing her eyes again and letting her thoughts drift. They drifted directly to Marsh, but she was too sleepy to fight it. She fell asleep, dreaming about the way he wore his hair and the shape of his chin—and the way he talked to her, sharing his secrets with her, sharing and showing her the warmth of his soul.

"Excuse me, miss."

The voice was deep and resonant and very male, but Leila was too tired to open her eyes. Besides, whoever he was, he probably wasn't talking to her. He was probably talking to someone else farther down the beach, and the wind was probably carrying his voice, making him sound as if he were standing right next to her.

"Miss, I couldn't help but notice that you've been asleep for nearly two hours," the voice said, "and the sun's way too hot to stay in one position like this and . . . Hey, aren't you Simon Hunt's sister?"

He *was* talking to her. Because as far as Leila knew, Simon didn't have any other sisters. She opened her eyes.

It was Hayden Young, suspected ninja and hunk lifeguard—live and in person and standing directly in front of her.

"Yes." Her voice sounded rusty from sleep, and she cleared her throat. She glanced over to where Frankie's chair had been, but the beach was empty. She vaguely remembered Frankie telling her good-bye, that it was time for her to go to work. "Simon's my brother. My name's Leila."

Hayden held out his hand. "Yep, I know." He gave her a smile worthy of a men's fitness magazine cover.

"You do?" Leila shook his hand. It was big. Big fingers, big palm. It engulfed hers almost entirely.

"Simon's mentioned you the few times we've talked," Hayden said. "And so has the town doctor—what's his name?—Devlin. Dr. Devlin. The Englishman." He didn't let go of her hand. Instead he tugged on it. "Come on. I'm on my way up to the concession stand. You should get out of the sun for a while and put some liquids into your system."

"All right." Leila let him pull her effortlessly out of her beach chair. This was perfect. Or almost perfect, anyway. It would be perfect if she could only think of a way to get him to kiss her. How on earth was she going to do that?

More than just Hayden Young's hands were big. Standing next to him, he was close to half a foot taller than she was, and even more muscular up close. With his long hair, he looked more like a professional wrestler than a philosophy doctoral candidate.

The effect of being pulled to her feet so suddenly after being sound asleep made her light-headed, and she swayed. Hayden reached out to steady her, putting his hands on her waist. His touch was extremely impersonal. In fact, it was remarkable how it *didn't* make her heart flutter.

"Yep, you definitely need some fluids." He kept one arm around her as they started up the beach.

Leila was grateful for his support but very aware of the many curious eyes watching them. "Careful." She glanced up at him. "You may want to grab hold of my elbow . . . or someplace a little less friendly looking. If we walk up the beach arm in arm like this, telephones all over Sunrise Key are going to start ringing."

Hayden grinned down at her. "I've noticed that gossip is a team sport here on the key. It doesn't take much to get those rumors flying, does it?"

Leila arched an eyebrow. "You sound like a man who's been burned."

"My third day on the key, I had lunch with Maggie O'Banyon. Do you know her? She works in that little souvenir shop on the road that leads out to the point?"

Leila nodded. "I know Maggie. Let me guess. You and Maggie had a friendly lunch, and by that evening, the entire town was planning your wedding."

"You got it." Hayden released her as they went under the open-air roof of the concession stand, watching her carefully to make sure she was all right. "Maggie was more upset about it than I was." He moved to the end of the refreshment line and took off his sunglasses. "I thought it was funny. But it seems she had been seeing a man who lived out on Captiva Island for quite some time, but no one knew. In order to kill the rumors about her and me, she had to tell everyone about this other guy."

"And you weren't upset by the rumors at all?"

"Like I said, it was funny. Although I have to confess, I haven't asked anyone to lunch since then. Or dinner either." He smiled. "I haven't wanted to risk starting any other rumors."

"I don't blame you." So much for kissing him. He may have put his arm around her, but he'd never in a million years kiss her right there on the public beach.

Oddly enough, Leila didn't care. It simply didn't matter. Despite the fact that Hayden Young was friendly and gorgeous, she couldn't picture herself falling in love with him. Even if he *was* her ninja and could kiss like a dream come true.

They'd reached the front of the line, and Hayden leaned on the counter, turning slightly to look back at Leila. "What'll you have?" he asked.

"I don't need anything," Leila said. "My purse is in the trunk of my car and—"

"My treat," Hayden offered. "What'll it be? Soda pop? Or a fruit slush? Or maybe some juice?"

She *was* thirsty. "A small ginger ale? No ice?"

"Make it a large," Hayden told the teenaged boy behind the counter. "And I'll have a large orange juice."

Leila leaned against the rough wood of the building's center support pole. She wasn't light-headed any longer, but she felt slightly odd. "I have to point out," she said to Hayden, "that you *have* risked starting another rumor by putting your arm around me on the beach, and now— horrors—by buying me a ginger ale. Don't you know that buying a woman a soda pop from the town beach concession stand is just a mere step away from buying her an engagement ring?"

Hayden laughed, his straight, white teeth gleaming. "If you want to know the truth, Leila, I figured you were safe."

Safe? What did he mean by *safe?* Safe enough to flirt with over a soda at the town beach? Or safe enough to kiss the heck out of at midnight on New Year's Eve?

"Everyone knows you've got something going with Dr. Devlin."

"Excuse me?"

He handed her an enormous paper cup of soda pop. "Uh-oh. Maybe that's just another rumor. You're *not* involved with the doctor?"

Leila sighed. "I wish," she murmured, voicing her thoughts before she stopped to think. Who was listening? She looked around, but although there were a number of covert glances being cast in their direction, no one was close enough to have heard her. Except, of course, Hayden.

He shook his head. "I don't get it. Dr. Devlin talks about you all the time. And I thought I saw you two together at Simon's party. Even if I hadn't heard the rumors, I would have thought . . ."

But Leila and Marsh had fought at Simon's party. Still . . .

"Really? Do you think . . . ?" My God, what was she doing, talking about her relationship with Marsh this way to a man who was almost a stranger?

"He's so reserved, so cool," Hayden said thoughtfully. "And maybe *that's* his problem. Maybe what he needs is to get heated up some." He smiled at her, a conspiratorial glint in his eyes. "I've got an idea."

Mary Lou Tennison's strident voice carried back from the reception area, into Marsh's office. With a sigh, he massaged his aching temples, then rose from behind his desk to shut the door. But before he even touched the doorknob, her words to Helen Burke, his nurse, caught his ear.

"And then," Mary Lou intoned, "Hayden Young *kissed* Leila Hunt. Right in the middle of the picnic area. Right on the mouth."

Marsh leaned his throbbing head against the doorframe, suddenly frightfully weary. Leila had done it. Somehow she'd managed to kiss the lifeguard.

"It wasn't just a little kiss," Mary Lou continued. "It was a very, very *big* kiss. Full body contact. The second hand on my watch went completely around the dial once . . . if not twice. It was like something out of *From Here to Eternity*, only without the rolling around in the surf. I nearly dropped the kids' fruit slushes on the floor."

Marsh started to close the door. God help him, he didn't need to hear this.

"And *then*," Mary Lou lowered her voice to a loud

stage whisper, "*She's* breathing hard, *he's* breathing hard, the entire concession stand is silent, you could have heard a pin drop, and he says—" she paused dramatically. Marsh found himself leaning out into the hallway. " 'When can I see you again?' "

Marsh closed his eyes as his head began to pound even harder. God, no. Sheriff Halliday hadn't really been a rival for Leila's affections, despite his good looks. But Young was bloody *perfect*. He was smart, handsome, and so damned nice it was sickening. If the lifeguard decided to pursue Leila, Marsh didn't stand a chance.

"What did Leila say?" Helen asked Mary Lou.

Marsh held his breath.

"She said, and I quote: 'You can see me whenever you want.' "

Marsh slammed the door.

When Leila got home from the town beach, there were two unfamiliar cars parked in the driveway. Visitors. Some of Simon's many friends, no doubt. His new girlfriend, Amanda, probably. But who else?

As she got out of her car, she stopped for a moment, feeling dizzy. The dull headache she'd been fighting ever since Hayden Young had woken her up on the beach suddenly exploded into full, pounding pain.

Leila went inside. The house was dark and cool, and her head should have felt better, but it still throbbed persistently. She needed some Tylenol, and a solid jolt of caffeine. She'd skipped her morning cup of coffee and she was paying for it now. With any luck, Simon had some cola stashed away in the fridge. The sound of voices and laughter came from the deck, and before she went into the kitchen, she went to investigate.

Simon was leaning against the railing, his arm around an ethereal-looking dark-haired woman who was gazing up at him with far too much adoration in her eyes. She had to be Amanda. She was younger than the women he usually dated, and her prettiness was more subtle, more delicate. She was wearing a long, loose, sleeveless dress that went all the way down to her ankles. She looked radiantly happy, poor thing.

Nancy Sullivan was sitting across the deck from them, nursing a tall glass of iced tea, and Leila stopped short in surprise.

"Hi." Nancy smiled. "I stopped in a little while ago, to see if you were around." She looked like the cat that had caught the canary. "I answered the phone while Simon was in the pool, and just so happened to speak with someone named Elliot?"

Elliot. "He called?"

"You didn't tell me you had a fiancé."

Leila shook her head. "He's not my fiancé—"

"Simon tells me that Elliot wants you to get married in New York City. He said that Elliot thinks a wedding reception is the perfect opportunity to schmooze with his clients. That is *the* most unromantic thing I've ever heard in my life. Leila, didn't you know that the wedding usually takes place in the bride's hometown?"

"I'm *not* getting married," Leila said, but no one seemed to be paying her much attention.

"I'm from Burlington, Vermont," Amanda volunteered. She pushed her glistening brown hair back from her face as she smiled up at Simon. "But I don't want to get married there. Ever since I was little, I've wanted to get married on the beach."

Leila caught Simon's eye and he squirmed slightly. Nothing like talk of marriage to make him want to run and hide. But somehow he remembered his manners and introduced Amanda to Leila.

"I don't think the wedding necessarily *has* to be in the bride's hometown," Nancy said. "But it *is* supposed to be the bride's choice. Her family throws and pays for the party, after all."

"I'd choose the beach," Amanda repeated. "Right here on Sunrise Key. It's so beautiful. . . . I could stay here forever."

"How about you, Simon," Leila asked her brother sweetly. "What do *you* think about getting married on the beach?"

Simon smiled weakly, well aware that Amanda was watching him. "To tell you the truth, I haven't really thought about it. It's going to be a long time before I get married. A *long* time."

But Amanda didn't look fazed, particularly when Leila said, "Si, I remember you saying what a great month April is here on the key. You said it was the perfect month to get married."

"At the time, I was talking about Noah and Kim Kavanaugh's wedding plans." Simon sent Leila a dangerous look.

"Oh, but I saw that envious look in your eye," Leila teased. She desperately needed that Tylenol, but the look on Simon's face was worth the wait. "And I caught you flipping through Kim's copy of *Modern Bride* magazine."

Her brother's eyes told her he wanted to wring her neck. But when he spoke, he said only one word. "Ninja." He said it softly but quite clearly.

"Excuse me?" said Nancy.

"Did you say *ninja*?" Amanda asked.

Simon was still looking at her, and Leila knew, without a doubt, that it was time to back down. "So, Nance." She turned to Nancy. "You have any plans for tonight?"

"Did I miss something?" Amanda asked, clearly confused.

"Actually, I was going to ask you if you wanted to go out and grab something to eat," Nancy said to Leila.

Amanda still looked perplexed. "What do ninjas have to do with *Modern Bride* magazine?"

Leila pulled a chair up next to Nancy's and sat down. "I don't know, Nance, I'm tired and kind of dizzy. I got too much sun today." Maybe she had some Tylenol in her beach bag. She searched through it quickly. No luck. "I think I'd rather stay in tonight. But you're welcome to stay for dinner." She looked at Simon. "What's on tonight's menu? More of those nasty little tofu hot dogs that you're so fond of?"

"Marsh is bringing home a couple of pizzas," Simon said. He looked at his watch. "Of course, if he's too much later, we'll have to call it breakfast."

"If you're sure there'll be enough, I'd love to stay," Nancy said.

"Wow, you're really sunburned," Amanda told Leila. "Did you spend *all* afternoon at the town beach?"

"Most of it."

"You went to the town beach?" Nancy asked, surprised. "Why? You have a terrific beach right here, inches from your house."

"Yes, Leila," Simon said pointedly, "why don't you tell us all why you went to the town beach this afternoon."

"Um, it was just a whim." She ignored Simon's wicked smile. "Frankie and I felt like going over there. We haven't been to the town beach in *years*, and . . ." She stood up. "Gee, will you look at the time! And I'm *covered* with sand." Simon's grin was triumphant as Leila beat a retreat. "I better take a shower before it gets too late."

Leila *was* sunburned. It didn't seem too bad, just enough to give her already tanned skin a reddish glow, and to make her feel hot. She lathered her body with lotion and got dressed, pulling on an oversized T-shirt and a loose-fitting pair of shorts.

As she went down the hall toward the stairs, she wobbled slightly. God, she was so hungry, she was lightheaded. Or maybe it was all that sun she'd had today. Whatever the case, all she wanted was to let the cool evening breeze soothe her warm face. And eat dinner. Except she was feeling a little queasy. But that was probably just the side effects of the aspirin she'd washed down with a can of cola after she searched to no avail for a bottle of nonaspirin pain reliever.

Leila carefully held the bannister as she went down

the stairs. As she crossed the foyer, she nearly ran smack into Marsh. Her heart soared crazily at the sight of him.

"Whoa." The short stop made her head pound almost as hard as her pulse. "Hi. If you're here, then pizza must be nearby."

He was still wearing his work clothes, and she watched as he tightened his tie around his neck and slipped back into his sports jacket.

"It's on the deck," he said shortly and went out the front door.

Leila followed him, standing with her bare feet on the warm asphalt of the driveway. "Marsh!" she called. "Aren't you going to have dinner?"

He turned back to look at her. His face was expressionless. "I seem to have lost my appetite."

She took a step toward him. "You're not still feeling the effects of last night, are you?"

Marsh laughed harshly. "Apparently last night had no lasting effect." His eyes were icy cold with anger. "To say I'm disappointed is an understatement. But you needn't worry. I received your message this time, loud and clear, thank you very much. I'll keep my distance from now on. And I'd appreciate it if you'd do the same. In other words, stay *out* of my affairs—financial or otherwise." He started down the driveway but turned back. "Oh, and I heard you found your ninja. Congratulations. I hope you'll both be very happy."

Leila stared at him blankly. His words didn't make sense. He was angry, but she didn't, for the life of her, know why.

He climbed into the jeep and, with an angry squeal of tires, drove away.

Hayden Young. Somehow Marsh had already heard about her staged encounter with the lifeguard. But that had almost been an afterthought. Most of his anger had been about something else. But what? Racking her brain, Leila went in search of Simon. Maybe he knew.

Simon was out on the deck, eating a slice of pizza. Leila pushed open the french doors and went outside and . . .

Nancy Sullivan was reaching into the pizza box for another slice.

Nancy Sullivan.

Oh, *shoot.* Leila's throbbing head pounded even harder.

Marsh thought Leila had invited Nancy over for dinner in order to play matchmaker. No wonder he was so angry. But he was wrong. True, Leila *had* invited Nancy to stay for dinner, but there had been no ulterior motive involved.

Because Leila, herself, was in love with Marsh.

That was what this was, this strange sensation, these feelings of euphoria combined with frustration and fear and hope. *That* was why one glance into Marsh's eyes made gravity disappear and her heart turn somersaults. It was *love.* After all these years of fighting tooth and nail, Leila had fallen completely, irrationally, passionately in love with Marsh.

True love.

With Marshall Devlin.

The light-headedness was back, full force. Leila closed her eyes and clung to the deck railing.

"Are you all right?" Nancy said. "You look a little green."

"I'm fine," Leila managed to say. She opened her eyes and looked up at Nancy. "Just a little dizzy. Too much sun and no lunch are a bad combination."

"Are you sure? Marsh was just here," Nancy told her, "but he had to go out again. Do you want me to try to catch him? Do you need a doctor?"

Leila did need a doctor. Specifically, a doctor named Marshall Devlin. But her needs had nothing to do with her light-headedness, and everything to do with her heart.

She shook her head. "I'm okay. Just hungry. Grab me a piece of pizza, pronto, can you?"

"Sure." Nancy returned in an instant, with a thick, cheesy slice on one of Simon's antique plates.

"This is *just* what I need," Leila said.

And everything went black.

NINE

"It's not heatstroke," Marsh said quietly to Simon as they stood outside of Leila's bedroom door. "Her temperature's not that severely elevated. But she does seem dehydrated. All her symptoms make me think it's heat exhaustion. And that could, of course, be a precursor to heatstroke. I'm going to sit with her awhile, force fluids."

Simon nodded. "Need any help? Forcing anything on Leila is next to impossible."

"Actually, I don't think it'll be a problem. She's been alarmingly acquiescent so far. Of course, she's mostly been asleep."

Leila was going to be fine. Marsh was the one who was going to need a week or so to recover. When Simon's phone number had come on his beeper along with the emergency code 911, Marsh had experienced sheer panic. He'd done a one-eighty on two squealing tires and prayed that it wasn't Leila who was injured—or worse.

When he'd seen Leila lying on the deck surrounded by Simon, his friend Amanda, and Nancy Sullivan, Marsh had known the true meaning of fear. It filled him from the inside out—a dark, deadly black cloud of terror that threatened to choke him. He knew then how much he loved this woman. He loved her enough to take a chance with her—to take on and prove wrong the prophecy of unhappily-ever-after that his parents' failed relationship had instilled in him.

Except, dammit, he was too late. Leila had found her dream lover in Hayden Young.

And last night Marsh had come close to flat out telling Leila that he loved her. He *had* told her that he wanted her, that he desired her. And what did she do? She invited her friend Nancy over for dinner in an attempt to fix him up.

That stung, like a hard, cold slap in the face.

Still, he'd nearly wept with relief as Leila roused slightly.

Marsh had carried Leila up to her bedroom and set to work cooling her down.

He stood talking to Simon now, shaking slightly from the adrenaline that had pumped into his system the second the message had appeared on his beeper.

"Call if you need help," Simon said.

Marsh nodded and went back into Leila's room with a bottle of Gatorade and a glass he'd brought upstairs from the kitchen.

Leila was asleep in the middle of her double bed. She

was sweating and restless and dangerously beautiful. He was there as her doctor; she was his patient. He was going to have to remember that.

Her blond curls were clinging to the sides of her face as Marsh lightly touched her cheek. She was still far too warm and damp.

He set the bottle and the glass on Leila's bedside table, then pulled the sheet off of her. Crossing the room, he turned on the fan in the far window, which sent a rush of cool ocean air across her body.

She was still wearing shorts and an oversized T-shirt. The shorts had an elastic waistband, and Marsh easily pulled them off, trying to make her a little cooler. It would have been better to take off her T-shirt, but he knew that she had nothing on underneath it.

Her panties were a deep, vibrant shade of blue, a mere wisp of silk and lace cut high on her legs. It figured she wouldn't be the demure white cotton type. Doctor, he thought. Not lover. Not tonight. Maybe not ever.

He sat down next to her, determined to ignore both his sudden despair and the bright blue splash of color.

She stirred again, and he touched her gently, pushing her hair from her face.

"Leila. Wake up for a bit, will you?"

Her eyelids fluttered open, but it took several seconds for her to focus on his face.

"Marsh." She gave him a sweet, warm smile that made Marsh's stomach hurt. Why couldn't she smile at him that way when she was fully conscious?

"Leila, you need something to drink," Marsh said as

her eyes closed again. "I need you to sit up for a sec and drink this."

"Fine," she mumbled, not moving. "That's fine, Marsh. Thanks."

"I'm going to help you sit up." Her only response was another weak smile.

"Right." He pulled her up and propped her back against his chest. She sagged like a rag doll. A *hot* rag doll. The body heat radiating from her was amazing. "Come on, love," he coaxed, holding the glass to her lips. "Drink up."

She took one sip and then another as he murmured encouragement. When she would have fallen back into bed, he still held her up. "A little more."

She took another long, deep drink, then turned her head to look up at him. "I *am* thirsty."

"That's splendid. Have some more."

"You know, I didn't invite Nancy for dinner." She was finally awake enough to hold the glass herself, and took another sip. "I mean, I *did*, but I didn't mean—"

"Shh. We don't need to talk about that right now. I forgive you, all right? Have some more—"

"No." She set the glass down on the bedside table. "There's nothing to forgive. Nancy stopped by. It was time for dinner. I asked her to stay. I didn't plan it. And as far as Hayden Young goes, I—"

"Leila, it's fine. Everything is fine, so stop worrying—"

"*You* stop patronizing me." She tried to pull away, but he held her tightly in place. There was no way he was going to let go of her. She'd fall directly on her head again.

"I'm *not* being patronizing."

"Yes, you are—"

"Right. You win. Now drink more of this. Please."

"You won't even let me explain." Tears filled her eyes, and Marsh knew he didn't stand a chance. One tear escaped and began to roll slowly down Leila's cheek.

"I'm sorry. I'm listening now, all right?"

"Nancy was here when I got home from the beach." Leila wiped at the tear. But another replaced it on her other cheek. "She wanted me to go out to dinner with her, but I was too tired. Simon said you were bringing home pizza, so I asked her to stay. I didn't stop to think you might jump to conclusions and get angry with me."

"Leila, love, I'm sorry. I thought . . . well, you know what I thought." Of course that didn't change what he'd overheard Mary Lou Tennison telling Helen Burke. His stomach still hurt to think about it.

Marsh poured more Gatorade into the glass and handed it back to her. "Drink," he ordered.

She took a sip, looking at him over the top of the glass. She was so enticingly beautiful. He could picture her with Hayden Young, his size-forty arms around her, two sets of blond hair moving gracefully in the breeze. She'd smile up at Young, her own violet-blue eyes sparkling with pleasure, and he'd bend his head to kiss her perfect, tantalizing lips—

"Do you want me to give Young a call?" Marsh worked hard to keep his voice even.

Leila frowned. "Who?"

"Hayden Young," he repeated, clearing his throat. "Your new boyfriend."

She handed Marsh the glass and sank back onto her pillows, eyes closed. "He's not my boyfriend. He wasn't my ninja, either."

"But—"

She opened her eyes and smiled drowsily at him. "I kissed him to make you jealous. He's nice, but he's not you."

Jealous? Marsh stared at Leila, trying desperately to process what she was telling him. She wanted to make him *jealous*? Good God! Did that mean . . . ?

She spoke again, but so softly that he couldn't hear the words.

"What was that?" Marsh leaned closer so that he could hear her.

"Did it work?" she breathed.

"Yes." He managed to speak despite the fact that his heart was lodged tightly in his throat.

"Good." Leila sighed, and Marsh leaned even closer to hear her. "I'm so tired. . . . I'm going to sleep now."

"All right. I'll be here if you need me. Just . . . I'll be here."

Leila smiled.

Her mouth was mere inches from his own. He was close enough to see the individual freckles that decorated her nose, close enough to smell the clean, sweet fragrance of her hair with each breath he took. One tear lingered on her cheek.

Marsh couldn't stop himself. He leaned forward, lightly kissing that last tear away.

But Leila turned her head and before he even realized what was happening, he was kissing her. He was kissing her sweet lips. Her mouth was warm, too warm. Her tongue was shockingly hot as she opened her mouth and—

Marsh's eyes flew open and he looked directly into the violet-blue swirls of Leila's eyes. He pulled back. "I'm . . . I'm sorry. I—"

"Don't stop, Marsh," she murmured, even as her eyes drifted shut.

Marsh's heart was pounding. She'd kissed him. *She'd* kissed him.

He made himself back away from the bed.

She'd kissed Hayden Young to make him jealous. She didn't think Young was her ninja.

He pulled the armchair next to her bed and sat down. He turned off the light and waited as his eyes grew accustomed to the soft moonlight streaming in through the windows. It bathed Leila with its silvery light, making her look angelic.

Marsh smiled.

He still had a chance. He had a chance, and he was going to do his damnedest to win Leila's heart. He had to.

Because tonight he'd had a very clear look at what losing Leila meant.

And he was damned if he was going to let that happen.

Leila spent the afternoon in the shade alongside the swimming pool. She'd slept away the morning, waking up well past noon.

Simon was out of town all day on business, but he called every few hours or so, checking in on her.

She was, she told her brother repeatedly, fine.

She had a very slight headache and was a little bit shaky, but other than that, she felt fine. Still, she followed the directions Marsh had scribbled on a piece of paper in his big blocky handwriting. Rule number one: Stay out of the sun. Rule number two: Push fluids. Rule number three: Take it easy.

And then there was rule number four: Have dinner with me tonight.

It wasn't a request. There wasn't a "please" in sight. That should have pushed all of the wrong buttons in Leila, but it didn't. As she looked at the message from Marsh for the tenth time that day, she didn't feel indignant or defensive. She felt only anticipation.

She remembered bits and pieces of her interaction with Marsh the night before. She remembered leaning against him as he coaxed her to drink cups and cups of that vile greenish juice. She remembered explaining why Nancy Sullivan was visiting. She remembered Marsh asking her if he should call Hayden Young. She remembered wanting to erase the grim look from his eyes, and telling him the truth about Hayden. She remembered him leaning forward to kiss her. . . .

But she didn't remember the kiss. Try as hard as she might, she could only recall up to the moment that his lips had met hers. Then it seemed to blur and blend with a dream she must've had the night before—a dream about her ninja.

Leila dove into the swimming pool, letting the water surround her, cocooning her in its cool stillness. She swam the length of the pool and back, and when she surfaced, the sunshine seemed unnaturally bright and the sound of her breathing and the splashing noises she made seemed too loud.

Why couldn't she remember Marsh's kiss?

She shook her wet hair back out of her face, and . . .

Leila froze—and dunked herself in the deep end. She came up sputtering and spitting water, and grabbed the side of the pool.

What if her memory of Marsh's kiss blurred and blended with her memory of her ninja's kisses because . . . Marsh *was* her ninja?

No. No, he couldn't be.

Could he?

Leila did a slow backstroke across the pool, staring up into the brilliant blue of the sky, trying to slow her racing heart.

If Marsh was her ninja, why hadn't he told her? Why had he let her go on this wild-goose chase? Why . . .

Leila suddenly became aware of a dark figure silhouetted against the sky at the edge of the pool. She stood up—the water was a little more than waist deep on this side. She shaded her eyes from the sun.

It was Marsh standing there.

His tie was loosened and the top button of his shirt was undone. His sleeves were rolled up to his elbows. He held his sports jacket by one finger over his shoulder.

Despite the fact that it was nearly eighty degrees in the shade, he looked his regular cool, collected self.

Except for his eyes.

They skimmed down the length of her body, lingering on her barely covered breasts, then even diving beneath the surface of the water. It was a wonder that the entire pool didn't begin to boil from the heat of his gaze.

Leila wrung the water from her hair, and his eyes followed her movement. He looked at her hands, her upraised arms, her breasts, her mouth, and then finally, *finally* into her eyes.

"You look like you're feeling much better."

She *had* been feeling better, but now she felt positively dizzy again. But it wasn't from heat exhaustion. Leila moistened her lips, and his eyes flickered to her mouth again. "I am." Her voice sounded husky.

Marsh nodded. "Good."

"You're home early." He was making her nervous. She sank down so that the water covered her to her neck. "Or are you still working? Is this a house call?"

Marsh swung his jacket off his shoulder and carried it over to one of the lounge chairs. "No." He turned back to her. "I'm quite done for the day. I left my black bag in the jeep." He glanced at his wristwatch. "As of five o'clock, the doctor is out. He can only be reached via beeper in the direst of emergencies."

"You have a beeper."

She was looking at him with the oddest expression on her face. Marsh watched as she swam gracefully toward the steps.

Water fell off her body in a sheet as she came out of the pool.

She was indescribably gorgeous. Marsh had never seen her wear this bathing suit before. It was black and tiny and it glistened from being wet—as did her tanned skin. It was remarkable—yesterday's sunburn had already turned to a delectable golden tan. She wore no makeup, and she looked clean and fresh and young.

But her pretty face and incredible body were all just decoration, wrapping for the vibrant, warm, amazing woman that Leila was. Marsh loved her so much at that moment, he couldn't speak.

She walked directly toward him.

Marsh had passed his anatomy classes at Harvard Med School with a 4.0 average. He'd learned the names of all of the muscles that tightened and relaxed and moved and flexed as Leila came toward him. But for the life of him he couldn't remember any of them right now.

All he could say was her name. "Leila . . ."

He'd fantasized all day, in between appointments, about coming home and pulling her close and kissing her until she melted in his arms. He'd fantasized about carrying her upstairs, into her bedroom, and making love to her as the sun set over the Gulf.

He'd fantasized about it, but knew it wasn't likely to happen. Leila probably had no idea what the sight of her in that skimpy bikini did to his blood pressure. She probably didn't realize that the look in her eyes was faintly predatory and made him nearly hum with desire.

Any second now, she'd get close enough to drip on

his shoes, flash him one of her magnificent smiles, and head for her towel.

But she didn't stop until her arms were around his neck, and her wet body was pressed tightly against him. He put his arms around her, too—he was no fool. He ran his hands up and down her back and arms, touching her, pressing her even closer to him.

She gazed up at him, and he knew she could see the shock in his eyes. She could probably see his desire, too, and if she couldn't see it, she could feel it from the proximity of their two bodies.

"Well," he said breathlessly, "this is quite a welcome home."

Leila gently pulled his head down and lifted her mouth to his and . . .

It was better than any of his fantasies. She kissed him slowly, sweetly, coaxing his mouth open with her tongue. Not that he needed coaxing. He met her tongue in a slow, sensual dance that made him feel drugged, intoxicated.

He heard himself moan, dizzy with emotion, and suddenly something flashed and the kiss was no longer slow, no longer languorous. The sweetness turned instantly to fire. Marsh could feel her body against his, white-hot and molten, her mouth granting him access, inviting him in. It was fierce and explosive, passionate and wild.

The entire world spun crazily as Marsh kissed Leila feverishly, deliriously. She angled her head to kiss him even harder, deeper. He thrust his fingers through her wet curls, burning with desire, giddy with love.

He loved Leila without reservation, without restraint. And he had to believe that she felt something for him, too. Because this time he wasn't wearing a mask. This time, she knew bloody well whom she was kissing.

And she was probably realizing right about now that he was . . .

Leila pulled back. Her breasts moved with every rapid breath she took, but Marsh couldn't look anywhere except into her eyes. She *knew*.

"You're my ninja."

Marsh nodded. "Yes."

"Oh, God."

He saw her hesitation, read the indecision in her eyes. She couldn't decide whether to yell at him or kiss him again.

He took the decision out of her hands, pulling her back into his arms and covering her mouth with his.

He would kiss her. He would kiss her until she forgot about being angry or hurt or upset or whatever she was feeling. He would kiss her, and then he would explain why he hadn't told her, and she would understand.

But she stiffened in his arms and pulled away.

"Leila," he started to say, and she pushed him, hard, into the swimming pool.

TEN

"Leila, dammit—*wait!*"

But Leila didn't want to wait. She grabbed her towel from the back of a chair and strode into the house, slamming the sliding glass door shut behind her.

She was halfway up the stairs before Marsh caught up with her. He was soaking wet and dripping all over Simon's rug. He pushed his hair back from his face. His eyes begged her to give him a chance, but the grim angle of his jaw told her he didn't truly expect her to.

"Leila, come on—"

He reached for her arm, but she pulled away, turning to glare down at him from several stairs higher.

"Why didn't you tell me?"

"It's rather hard to explain, but—"

"I'll bet it's hard to explain." The hurt she was feeling threatened to overpower her, to make her dissolve into tears. How could he have done this to her? How could he have watched for nearly two weeks while she

made a royal fool of herself? She had been so stupid—
she hadn't even suspected Marsh. But now that she
knew, it all made perfect sense. Marsh wore a beeper.
Kim Kavanaugh had gone into hard labor right around
midnight. . . .

She could imagine Marsh and Simon, reduced to a
puddle of tears, laughing at her behind her back. The
image stung and burned. She couldn't bear the hurt, so
she focused on the anger. She crossed her arms and
spoke through clenched teeth. "Clearly, you intended to
humiliate me right from the start."

"It's hard to explain, but if you let me, I'll try—"

"Did you and Simon have a good laugh?"

"Of course not," Marsh said indignantly. "We didn't
laugh—"

"Oh, God. Simon *did* know." She scrambled up the
stairs, desperate to get away from him, afraid that any
moment she was going to burst into tears.

On the top landing, Marsh caught her arm. "Leila,
please—"

"Leave me alone! The joke's over. You win."

"It wasn't a joke. It wasn't any kind of joke."

She whirled to face him, poking him in the chest
with one finger. "Somehow, some day, I'm going to get
back at you for this, Devlin. I'm not sure how, but you
better believe that I'll think of something."

She turned to run to her room because the tears were
coming and dammit, there was nothing she could do to
stop them.

But Marsh still held her arm, and he didn't let go. He
gripped both of her shoulders, forcing her to look at

him—forcing her to let him see just how badly he had hurt her.

Tears spilled down her cheeks as the pain broke through the last of her fragile defenses. To her complete horror, she couldn't hold back the deep, body-shaking sobs that seemed to rip through her.

Marsh was stunned. Leila was crying. She was crying as if her very heart had been ripped from her chest and stomped into a thousand tiny pieces.

"Don't cry! Leila, please, I promise you, I wasn't trying to trick you, or play a joke on you, or anything. I didn't tell you I was the man you were looking for, because I thought you'd run away from me."

She pulled free from his grasp, and ran for her room.

"Exactly the way you're running right now." Her door slammed shut. He cursed in frustration as he tried the doorknob. It was locked.

But his room was next to hers—they shared the same balcony. Marsh went into his bedroom and out the balcony door. Leila's door was open. He knocked on the frame as he opened the screen door.

"Leila?"

She was sitting on her bed, her back to him. If she was still crying, her tears were silent now. "Go away."

"I can't." He sighed. "I need to make you understand."

"I understand. I understand that you're a bastard." She laughed, but her voice was still thick with tears. "You know, I was actually starting to fall in love with you. What a fool."

"But, that's what I wanted."

"Then you're even more cruel than I thought." Leila stood up, squaring her shoulders and wiping her eyes on the heels of her hands as she turned to face him. "I'd like you to leave."

"I wanted you to fall in love with me," Marsh said desperately, "because—" he took a deep breath, "because *I'm* rather frantically in love with *you*."

Leila's eyes widened. "You *love* me?" she whispered.

"Yes." The word was easier to say than he'd imagined. It was almost laughably easy to say because Leila was standing there looking at him, the hurt in her eyes disappearing with every word he spoke. "I've been in love with you for about as long as I can remember. It seems to be something of a terminal condition," he admitted with a small smile.

But Leila didn't smile back at him.

"Really?" she asked.

Marsh met her gaze steadily, for the first time in his life dropping all of his defenses, letting Leila see, *really* see into his soul, into his heart. It was terrifying—and exhilarating. "Yes," he whispered.

Marsh didn't know who moved first, but he met Leila halfway, and then she was in his arms again, and he was kissing her and she was kissing him.

She believed him. Thank God. Thank *God*.

He kissed her again and again, for what seemed like an eternity. Her mouth was so soft. Her skin was so smooth, and there was so much of it that wasn't covered by her bathing suit.

Marsh finally knew the true meaning of ecstasy.

And then Leila pulled him back with her onto her bed, wet clothes and all.

This couldn't possibly be happening. It was everything he'd ever wanted, all of his fantasies coming true.

She kissed him again, a feverish, scorching kiss that left him dizzy with desire. She began to move, sliding her body along the growing length of his arousal, hooking her legs around him, fitting him even more tightly against her.

He was going to make love to Leila. Right here. Right now. The realization spun him around and damn near knocked him over.

She tugged at his wet shirt and he moved back. One swift yank pulled it up and over his head. Her top followed, and then she was in his arms, wearing only those dangerously tiny bathing suit bottoms.

Her breasts were perfect. Small and firm, they fit his hands perfectly. He kissed her fiercely, trying to show her how he felt, trying to show her the total and absolute power she had over him.

He trailed kisses down her neck, down to the hard pink buds of her nipples, taking first one and then the other into his mouth. She moaned and he suckled harder until she cried out. Marsh ran his hands up and down and across her stomach and back and breasts and thighs, kissing her and caressing her with his mouth and tongue and fingers until she all but shook with desire.

His hand swept underneath the black nylon of her bathing suit and she arched up against him, pressing his fingers deep inside of her.

He felt her hands fumble with his belt buckle, felt

her loosen the belt, unbutton and unzip his pants. He clenched his teeth, hard, to keep from crying out as her fingers closed around him.

Yes. *Yes.* This was what he'd wanted for so long. A chance to be one, to be joined with this woman that he loved so desperately. She was watching him, smiling at his reaction to her exquisite touch.

She released him, but only to pull off her bathing suit. She wiggled free, and then she was gloriously naked.

And his. All his.

His wet pants stuck to his legs, but he peeled them off in record time.

Miraculously, the single condom he carried in his wallet went on easily. Leila lay back in her bed, watching him. And if she knew that it had been a great deal of time since he'd used a condom—since he'd had the opportunity or even desire to use one—she kindly didn't comment.

She just smiled at him.

And reached for him as he turned toward her, welcoming him back to her with a kiss that made his head spin. She wrapped her legs around him, pulling him close, eagerly pressing herself against him.

"For the record," he said hoarsely, pulling back very slightly, "I *do* love you rather desperately. So if I begin to weep or utterly lose control, you'll know why."

Her eyes filled with tears. "Marsh—"

"Shh." He kissed her. "Don't say a word. You don't have to say a single word. Just let me love you."

She kissed him again, arching herself against him in a silent plea. Now. She wanted him now.

"Look at me, Leila," he commanded.

She met his gaze, catching her breath as he slowly, tenderly, exquisitely guided himself deep within her, filling her completely.

"Oh," she breathed.

He was one with Leila. Both physically and emotionally, Marsh was complete as he'd never been complete before.

He began to move, slowly, deliberately, still holding her gaze. She moved then, too, savoring each thrust, each delicious wave of sensation.

It was entirely possible that he was not going to live through this experience. It was too perfect, too intense. His heart felt swollen and heavy and damn near ready to burst. But if he died now, God knows he'd die a happy man.

Beneath him, Leila moved faster, harder, and he kissed her, matching her movements, picking up the pace. He felt her long, graceful fingers sweeping down his back, her hands cupping his buttocks, holding him more tightly inside her. His skin was slick with perspiration, but she didn't seem to care, in fact, she caught a bead of moisture that ran down his neck with her tongue, damn near pushing him over the edge into oblivion.

Marsh fought for precious control as he gazed down at her. He wanted to shout that she belonged right there, on Sunrise Key, in his arms forever and ever. She didn't think she could be happy living on Sunrise Key? Well, right this very moment, she was looking happily-ever-after straight in the eye.

She pulled him down, so that the full weight of his body was on top of her. Her breath came in gasps, and he could feel the wonderful contrast of her soft breasts and pebble-hard nipples against his chest. She drew his tongue deep into her mouth, moaning her pleasure.

Marsh felt the first wave of her release as she clung to him. She wanted more, *more*, so he gave it to her. And then, as the turbulence of her climax grew, he gave her everything. He relinquished his tenuous control and joined her, rocketing up into a wild, delirious explosion of colors and sounds and sensations.

She owned him, body, heart, and soul.

He could only pray that she felt the same.

"Leila, love, I've got to go."

The man in the ninja costume gently brushed Leila's hair from her face and then kissed her. It was another of his deep, soulful kisses, the kind that made her melt.

Leila put her arms around his neck, holding him tightly. "Don't go. Stay."

He kissed her again. His mouth was cool and fresh and tasted like toothpaste. "You know I'd love to stay," he murmured. "But Megan Andrews is running a temp of one-oh-four and her parents are already waiting for me in the office and—"

Leila opened her eyes, suddenly wide awake, suddenly remembering everything, *everything* that had transpired late the day before. And the night.

Marsh.

Marshall Devlin was her ninja. Marshall Devlin was the man who had kissed her at Simon's New Year's Eve party.

He was also the man who had made love to her most exquisitely, nearly all night long.

". . . a message from Matt Lenore on my answering service. No doubt he forgot to change the dressing on his burned hand and now it's probably infected." Marsh was sitting on the edge of her bed, one arm braced on either side of her. "I may as well have him come into the office while I'm there. Save me a house call later tonight."

His hair was still wet from his shower, and he wore a clean white shirt and a pair of dark blue pants. He looked more like the Marsh Devlin she thought she'd known all these years than the man who had made such incredible, passionate love to her. Except his eyes were so warm as he looked down at her, so hot with the memories of the love they'd shared.

His hair fell into his eyes, and Leila found herself reaching up and gently pushing it back. He took her hand and kissed it.

"I'll come home as soon as I can. Take it easy again today. Be careful of the sun. Stay cool. In fact, stay in bed." The heat in his eyes turned hotter. "Save my place. With any luck, I'll be back in just a bit, all right?"

He didn't wait for her to answer. He kissed her again, lightly this time, and left the room, closing the door gently behind him.

Marsh was her ninja.

The concept was still shocking.

The night before, after Marsh had told her that he loved her, she hadn't thought once about the fact that he was her mystery man.

Oh, the way he'd made her feel!

It was frighteningly intense. It was frighteningly powerful. It was frighteningly real.

It was frighteningly *frightening*.

What a mess this was turning out to be.

She'd always been convinced that Marsh looked down his nose at her. Now he claimed to be in love with her. And God knows she was head-over-heels in love with him. But what did it all mean? As far as she could see, being in love with Marsh only complicated her life beyond belief.

He lived in Florida; she lived in New York. How the heck were they going to make *that* work? Compromise, and live in North Carolina?

No, it would be unfair to ask Marsh to leave Sunrise Key. He *loved* it there. And over the past week and a half, Leila had gotten a real reminder of what there was to love about this place.

It was more than the turquoise water and the clean, white sand. It was more than the weather and the waves. It was the community, the town, the odd collection of people who had become Marsh's friends.

On the other hand, the small size of the town didn't allow for the sense of anonymity that Leila felt living in New York City. On Sunrise Key, all you had to do was sneeze loudly, and you'd receive five get-well cards in the next day's mail.

Face it, for all its charm and friendliness—or maybe *because* of its friendliness—Sunrise Key had an absolute dearth of privacy. Particularly since Simon, the nosiest brother this side of the Mississippi, lived there.

Simon . . .

Leila sat up.

He had known right from the start that Marsh was her ninja. He had known . . . and he hadn't said a word.

Leila pulled on her bathrobe and tied the belt tightly around her waist. She ran a brush quickly through her hair, and then went out into the hall.

Simon's bedroom door was open a crack, and she peeked in. His bed was empty but obviously slept in. Despite the early hour, he was awake.

She went down the stairs and into the kitchen.

Her brother was standing at the counter, cutting himself a slice of watermelon. He looked at her in surprise.

"What are *you* doing up?" he asked. "I thought Dev told you to take it easy again today."

"You knew," she said, narrowing her eyes at him.

"Knew what? You know, you scared us all to death. Since when do you pass out from too much sun? You were always the kid who could outlast any of us when it came to sunbathing. Shame on you for proving you're human." He took a bite of watermelon for punctuation.

"I can't *believe* you knew all along that Marsh was the ninja, and you didn't tell me," she shouted.

"He asked me not to," Simon defended himself, holding his watermelon like a shield. "He told me in confidence. I couldn't turn around and tell *you.*"

Leila sat down at the kitchen table. "I feel like such a fool."

"Hey." Simon took the last bite of his watermelon and tossed the rind into the garbage. "If you want *my* take on the situation, Marsh found it impossible to walk up to you and just blurt out the truth." He rinsed his hands in the sink, looking over his shoulder at her. "*I* would've found it tough to do, and Marsh is a hundred thousand times more bottled up than I am. I mean, can you picture him just walking up to you and saying, 'Oh, by the way, I love you'?"

Leila shook her head.

"Yet at the same time," Simon continued, drying his hands on a towel, "without getting into any of the intimate details of what went down last night, I've got to believe that Marsh must have made *some* mention of love and—"

"Whoa." Leila held up one hand. "Last night? What do *you* know about what happened last night?"

Simon shrugged. "Obviously Marsh told you the truth and nature took its course. I'm happy for you both."

"Oh, perfect." Leila raised her eyes to the ceiling. "Marsh *told* you about last night? That's absolutely perfect. Do you suppose there's anyone in town who hasn't heard about it yet?"

Simon sat on the kitchen counter, directly in front of her. "Don't be an idiot." He crossed his arms and looked down at her. "Dev didn't say a word. He's not the kind to kiss and tell."

"Then how do you know I . . . that 'nature took its course'?" Leila demanded. Her face flushed with embarrassment.

"I know because I answered the phone when Ed Andrews called about Megan's fever at six-thirty," Simon said evenly. "I went to Dev's room to wake him up, but he wasn't there. I went into your room, thinking he'd fallen asleep in the chair, the way he did the night before, when you were sick. He was there, and he was asleep all right, but he wasn't in any chair. He was in the bed. With you. And it was quite clear that he wasn't acting in the capacity of your personal physician. Sorry if I infringed on your privacy, Lei."

"What privacy? There *is* no privacy on Sunrise Key. And there's certainly no privacy in your house!"

"I honestly didn't know you guys were . . . you know. Involved." He smiled and Leila wanted to punch him. This is what it would be like, living here. Everything she did, every move she made, somehow Simon would find out about it. God forbid she ever got pregnant. No doubt Simon would somehow find out the test results before she did.

"I have to confess," he added, "that I'm really glad you're not going to marry that bozo, Elliot—"

"But I am," Leila lied, wanting to wipe Simon's smug smile off his face. "I'm going back to New York City where privacy isn't a miraculous occurrence. I have to tell Elliot what happened, of course. But if Elliot will still have me, I *am* going to marry him."

It worked. Simon's smile was gone.

There was a pay phone on the corner in front of the gas station. It was a secure line. There was no chance of Simon or anyone else overhearing her call. And that was good, because this was not a call that was going to be any fun to make.

She dialed Elliot's office in New York and waited while his secretary patched her through to his desk.

He sounded rushed and didn't seem to notice or particularly care when Leila told him she was thinking about spending another week or so down on Sunrise Key. So she went a step further, and told him that she'd decided not to marry him.

He stopped shuffling the papers on his desk for all of seven seconds. But he bounced back quickly, wishing her all the best, telling her to stay in touch.

Leila slowly hung up the phone. The call was over. The relationship was done. Just like that.

She wished Marsh could be handled as easily. She wished her heart wasn't involved. She wished she could just call him up and say, "Sorry, bad mistake." But she couldn't. Because if her night with Marsh had been a mistake, it was the best mistake she'd ever made.

Never before had she felt so cherished, so loved. Never before had she felt so in tune with another person. Never had she felt so completely happy.

Despite everything she'd said to Simon, the real

truth was that Leila was actually considering moving back home to Sunrise Key. Her career wouldn't suffer that much. She'd only lose maybe a third of her clients if she played her cards right. The others would stick with her, particularly if she reduced her rates. And the cost of living was lower down here. She'd probably wind up ahead in the long run.

Still, the idea of coming back to this small town, of moving back to her childhood home, was frightening.

She wanted Marsh's love, but at what price?

And when the time came, would she be willing to pay it?

When Leila returned to Simon's house, he met her at the door.

"Who let *you* out? You're supposed to be taking it easy again today."

She brushed past him, and he closed the screen door behind her. "I didn't realize I was being held prisoner," she retorted. All of her confusion and doubt and frustration was instantly redirected as anger—anger at her brother. After all, this mess was partially his fault. If he had told her the truth about her ninja right from the start . . .

"Did you talk to Dev?" Simon asked. His normally serene blue eyes were icy and crystalline.

Leila crossed her arms. "No."

Simon crossed his arms, too, undaunted. "If you're really leaving in three days with the intention of marrying Elliot the clown, you probably shouldn't wait until the last moment to discuss this with Marshall."

Leila went into the kitchen. "I don't need you to butt in. In fact, you better not, or—"

Simon laughed as he followed her. "Too late." He jumped up and sat on the kitchen counter. "I've already butted in. I told Dev what you told me."

Leila spun to face him. If he'd told Marsh that she was going to marry Elliot anyway, Marsh would think that the night they'd spent together had meant nothing to her. "I can't believe you did that!"

"If you drop a bomb, kiddo, you have to deal with the fallout. Dev happens to be my friend. I figured you were about to emotionally eviscerate the man, and I thought at least by giving him a warning, I might be able to make the event a little less painful."

"Emotionally eviscerate? Who said anything about emotional evisceration?" Leila said. "I wasn't serious about marrying Elliot, you idiot! I was just trying to make you mad."

"So what are you saying? That you're going to marry Dev?"

"He hasn't exactly asked." Leila turned away from him.

"Give him half a second and less than half a chance and he will."

Leila took a bottle of seltzer from the refrigerator. Her hands were shaking as she poured herself a glass. She took a sip before she spoke.

"I don't think he will. I think he knows as well as I do that there's no real future in our relationship."

"There can be," Simon said. "It just depends on how far you're willing to go. It depends on the risks you're willing to take to make it work."

"Moving back home isn't any kind of risk."

"Maybe you have to stop thinking about it as moving *back* home." Simon slid off the kitchen counter. "You're really moving ahead—your destination just happens to be Sunrise Key. And Marsh Devlin. Maybe you should try thinking of it *that* way."

He ruffled her hair as he left the kitchen.

Marsh wasn't in his office downtown.

But Leila ran into Frankie on the sidewalk in front of his office building.

"Hey, I heard you did a nosedive onto the deck a few nights ago."

Leila looked at her friend. Frankie's shiny black hair was damp with perspiration, and she was wearing a torn T-shirt and a pair of paint-splattered cutoffs that had seen better days. "You must've been talking to Nancy Sullivan."

Frankie sat down on the hood of Leila's car and fanned herself with the file folder she was carrying. "Actually, I heard it from Jeanette Miller who heard it from Laura Beauchamp who got it directly from Nancy."

"God, is nothing secret around here?" Leila let her annoyance slip through. "Does the entire town know?"

"Yep," Frankie said cheerfully. "And there's a betting pool on the baby's due date."

Leila's mouth dropped open in surprise. "They all think I'm . . ."

"Preg-o." Frankie grinned. "Can't pass out around here without a group discussion afterward. The majority consensus is that you're With Child. Capital *W*, capital *C*."

Leila groaned.

"Of course, the fact that your alleged fiancé-to-be was a no-show at the biggest party of the year is adding a slice of intrigue to all of the speculation," Frankie continued. "Especially since Paul Casella swears he saw a woman who looks an awful lot like you practicing mouth-to-mouth with Liam Halliday one evening last week, out on the corner of Ocean Avenue and Main Street."

"Oh, damn."

"And just this morning I ran into ol' Liam. Apparently the rumor that he's fathered your illegitimate child is spreading like wildfire. He's looking for you, wants to talk. I think he's worried."

"Worried about *what?*" Leila sputtered. "Surely he knows that one kiss doesn't get a woman pregnant."

Frankie shrugged. "How's he know he didn't bed you in some drunken fog? For all he knows, he *did* get you pregnant."

"This is terrific. This is *really* terrific."

"Of course, there's the contingent who's certain the baby's Marshall Devlin's. Ellen Hartman is positive she saw you kissing Marsh at Simon's New Year's Eve party—right before Marsh took off his *ninja costume* and went to go deliver Kim Kavanaugh's baby."

Leila glanced at her friend, who was watching her closely.

"You already knew," Frankie said. "You knew Marsh was your ninja."

Leila nodded.

"You knew because you kissed him, right?"

Leila nodded.

"Ah-ha. Just as I suspected. Kissed him and maybe, um . . . ?"

Leila closed her eyes. "Too much sun. I fainted from too much sun. I'm not going to have Marsh Devlin's baby or Liam Halliday's baby or *anyone's* baby."

"And you kissed Marsh Devlin because . . . ?"

"Why do *you* kiss a man, Frankie?"

Frankie's grin broadened. "Either because I'm wildly attracted to him . . ."

"Well, there you go."

"Or because I'm in love with him?"

It was a question Leila didn't want to answer. But Frankie was watching her intently, reading every flash of emotion that crossed Leila's face.

"I knew it."

"Don't you dare tell *any*one."

Frankie made a zipper motion across her mouth.

Yeah, right. Leila gave it exactly fifteen minutes before the entire town knew that she was in love with Marsh Devlin.

"This small-minded, gossip-mongering, no-privacy, stupid little town is driving me *insane*," Leila fumed.

"It's not *that* bad."

"You're not the one everyone thinks is pregnant."

"Oh, that's just talk. They're not being malicious, just curious. Interested, if you please," Frankie said. "They'll all get over it."

"When?"

"As soon as the next good topic of conversation comes around. Simon and Amanda, for instance. Simon's within a few days of jettisoning Amanda. I can tell by the look in his eyes when he's out with her. There's lots of white showing. She's starting to talk about 'we' this and 'our' that and he's running scared. As soon as they split, everyone'll stop talking about you. Guaranteed."

"Great," Leila grumbled. "If it's not one Hunt providing townwide entertainment, it's another. Oh, Frankie, how did I get myself into this?"

"Into what?" Frankie asked. "You're nuts about Marsh, he's nuts about you. Ninety-nine percent of the population is trying to get into a situation like that. You should be happy."

"But the thought of moving back here . . ."

"Yeah, imagine being able to hang out with *me* whenever you felt like it. *That* would be the real pits."

"I didn't mean that."

"Sunrise Key isn't exactly one of Dante's levels of hell, Lei. Some people actually *want* to live here. Back when we were kids, you liked living here."

"I grew out of it," Leila muttered.

"Are you sure? Or did you just get temporarily sidetracked? Remember how you always used to say that when you had kids someday, you wanted to give 'em a chance to grow up in a small town like this? Do you really want to raise your children in a city?"

Leila was silent.

"There may be no privacy here," Frankie pointed out, "but there's also no crime. And no snow. And no pollution. And no traffic jams. . . . You feel up to taking a ride?" Frankie asked. "I want to show you something."

Leila looked over at her friend. "What?"

Frankie smiled. "I want to give you a reminder about the good side of living on Sunrise Key."

Leila heard the sound of buzz saws and hammers from inside Frankie's pickup truck as they drove down Point Road. Frankie drove slowly, squeezing through the lines of cars and trucks that were parked along both sides of the narrow street all the way to the corner.

"What's going on?" Leila asked. "What's happening?"

And then Frankie rounded the curve and pulled up in front of Marsh's house.

It was amazing.

The last time Leila was there, the house had been a sagging pile of rubble and ashes. But now, the burned-out shell was down, the foundation cleaned out, and a brand new, fresh wood frame was already up.

She could see Ron Hopkins, still on crutches, standing beside a truckful of wood, supervising five strapping teenaged boys—his sons—who were unloading it. Duke Torrelson and Kevin Beauchamp were up on the roof, nailing down the sheathing. Axel Bayard, Noah Kavanaugh, John Knudsen, and about ten men and women Leila didn't recognize were hammering the studs and beams of the inside partition walls into place. John McGrath, Nancy Sullivan, and Kelly Beauchamp were constructing the stairs up to the second floor. Liam Halliday and several uniformed policemen were framing off the windows and doors. Dozens of other people, many of whom Leila didn't know, swarmed over the structure.

It was good, old-fashioned barn raising. Well, a *house* raising in this case. The entire town was pitching in, doing the work, rebuilding Marsh's house.

"This was actually Marsh's idea." Frankie pulled her truck into a space recently vacated by a departing car. "The electrician and the plumber are going to do the work for a discount, and everyone else is working for free—even the architect, courtesy of Pres Seaholm. Marsh is giving everyone in town a chance to pay off all their debts to him. But to tell you the truth, I think everyone'd be here regardless of that. In fact, I see a lot of people who don't owe Marsh Devlin one cent. But on Sunrise Key, it's not a matter of who owes what to whom. It's a matter of being a good neighbor and a good friend. Marsh is both of those things to everyone in town."

Marsh had always talked about investing in people. Leila realized she was looking directly at the payoff.

She cleared her throat to get rid of the lump that had suddenly appeared. "Did he know this was happening today?"

Frankie shook her head. "No. We didn't know ourselves—not until the supplies came in this morning. The weather forecast calls for no rain for the next five days, so we figured we'd get started." She looked back at the house. "If we keep up this pace, the exterior will be completed well before that, even though most of the work will be done in the evening, after the regular workday. The inside'll take a little longer, because of the plumbing and wiring, but . . ." She shrugged. "Marsh's jeep is in the driveway, so I guess he's here somewhere. He's probably really happy."

Leila shielded her eyes with one hand, searching for Marsh's familiar brown hair.

"I'm going to get back to work," Frankie continued. "If you want to pitch in, talk to Pres. He's assigning jobs."

Leila watched as Frankie joined the team building the inside stairs.

Back when we were kids, you liked living here, Frankie had reminded her. And suddenly, in a rush, it all came back, the feelings of intense happiness she'd had as a child, the sunshine-swept days and warm tropical nights, surrounded by friends and laughter.

All of these people were going to spend the better part of their time off over the next few weeks right here, helping a beloved neighbor. It was old-fashioned and sweet, and it made Leila's chest ache. She could see friendship on every smiling face—and even on the frowning ones. Axel Bayard was arguing with his old friend John Knudsen, but their affection for each other was evident even in their raised voices.

She'd never seen anything remotely like this in her uptown Manhattan neighborhood.

And she probably never would.

It was true that in New York, she wouldn't have dozens of nosy neighbors betting on the due date of her nonexistent baby.

But she also wouldn't have Marsh.

Marsh.

He was here somewhere.

Leila went to look for him.

Marsh stood alone on the beach, looking out over the ocean. Up above him, on the bluff, the newly constructed frame of his house loomed. He could hear the sound of hammers and saws, the sound of voices and laughter.

The water sparkled in the early afternoon sunshine. Seabirds soared and dipped, their raucous cries muted by the sound of the gentle surf.

Ever since he first came to Sunrise Key, Marsh had loved the view from this part of the island. He used to rent one of the dilapidated touring bikes from Millie's Market for his entire vacation, and ride out every day with a book to read and his lunch in a paper sack. He'd sit for hours, not too far from this very spot, looking out at the ocean, feeling the warmth of the sun on his face, breathing in the fresh, salty air—and healing.

He'd come to accept the fact that his mother was gone. He'd loved her, but she was gone. There was nothing he could do—except learn to live without her.

It had taken some time. Time, and the brilliant turquoise-blue vastness of the Gulf, the sparkling white at the edge of the water, the healing power of the sun, the soothing sounds of the wind and waves and gulls.

On Sunrise Key, Marsh had left the last of his childhood behind him. He'd let go of the bitter anger he'd felt toward his mother for deserting him the way she had. He'd made the decision to move forward, to embrace his future rather than linger in the past, defeated by grief and disappointment. He'd found peace and security, and eventually a real sense of belonging.

True, his life wasn't perfect by any means. Financially, he was earning far less than he'd been accustomed to having as a child and a teenager. And the fire had been a rather nasty blow. But he had more friends than he could count on all of his fingers and all of his toes.

Marsh looked up at the house, at the walls and roof that were going up. They were tangible proof of his strong and lasting friendships with the people of Sunrise Key.

He looked back at the ocean, at the incredible, splendid view. Yes, this was right where he'd always wanted to be.

Except Leila wasn't with him. And deep down inside, he knew that all the water, sand, sun, wind, and time that Sunrise Key had to offer wouldn't help him learn to live without *her*. It wouldn't help him one bit this time.

And whether or not Leila loved him, he knew he really had only one choice.

With one last look back at the house, Marsh flipped open the cellular phone that Preston Seaholm had lent him.

It was time to make a few phone calls to some old

med school friends. It was time to call in a few favors, make a few new connections, and find himself a new job.

In New York City.

Preferably within walking distance of Leila's uptown apartment.

Because if Leila was going to get married, she wasn't going to marry Elliot. She was going to marry *him*.

ELEVEN

Leila couldn't find Marsh.

She searched the construction site but didn't see him until he stood in the center of the newly constructed plywood floor of his house and called for his friends and neighbors' attention.

"Thank you," he said loudly as the group quieted down to listen to him. "First of all, I'd like to thank you all for coming over here today. Your kindness is deeply appreciated, and I will always remember it. However . . ."

He sighed, looking around at all of the different faces in the crowd. His eyes fell on Leila, and he started in surprise. But he held her gaze, his eyes almost challenging as he said. "However, I'm going to be leaving Sunrise Key—"

"No!" The word was out of Leila's mouth before she even realized it. All eyes turned to look at her.

"Yes," Marsh chided her gently. "I'm moving to New York. It really wasn't that difficult a decision."

The crowd murmured its displeasure at the news, and Leila took the opportunity to cross the room toward Marsh.

"You can't be serious about this."

"I'm dead serious," he replied. "If you're going back, I'm following. I haven't quite figured out what to do about Elliot, but I'm working on it."

His eyes swept her face, then lower before returning to her eyes. Leila knew that if they hadn't been standing in front of an audience, he would have taken her into his arms and kissed her.

"There's no way I'm going to let you get away from me," he said as if he were discussing the weather. "Not after last night."

The crowd was silent again, hanging on his every utterance—despite the fact that Marsh's voice was lowered and his words were meant to be private. He realized what he'd just said and winced. "Sorry," he murmured to Leila.

She closed her eyes. "It doesn't matter. They all probably know anyway," she whispered.

"Regardless, I *am* going to New York."

"We need to talk about this." She glanced around at all the curious faces. "Privately."

Marsh raised his voice so everyone could hear him. "I'd like to thank you all again, but please, there's no need to do any more work here. You may as well go home."

Leila raised her voice, too. "Nobody move. There's

still a few hours of daylight left, and a lot of work to do over the next few days. Dr. Devlin is having a temporary problem with reality. He's not going to New York or anywhere else—"

"I most certainly am," Marsh interrupted indignantly. "I love you, and—"

"Please," Leila said desperately to the crowd. "Just go back to work."

"What, and miss this?" Millie Waters called out. "This is better than *Melrose Place*."

The crowd laughed, and nobody left. Several people sat down, making themselves more comfortable, and others moved to where they could see better. Leila groaned.

"I've made up my mind," Marsh told her.

"Atta boy, Doc," John Knudsen called out. "You love her, you follow her to Siberia if you have to."

Leila put her hands on her hips and glowered at John Knudsen. "Oh, that's really intelligent. He's just supposed to follow me, huh? No job, no money—you know, it takes a lot of money to live in New York City."

"She's got a point," Axel Bayard said to John.

"But I have got a lead on a job," Marsh announced. "A friend of a med school friend joined his father's private practice—GP—after his residency. Apparently, the old man had a heart attack about four months ago. He's got to take it easy, retire, and that's left the son working eighteen-, twenty-hour days to keep up with the patient load."

Marsh turned toward Leila. "I made a reservation on the same flight you're taking on Sunday," he continued.

"I'm going to meet with the son—his name's Grant Osgood, he was two years ahead of me at Harvard—and discuss the possibility of joining him as a partner in the practice. Glen—my friend—thinks Osgood and I will hit it off. If he's right, I'll be living up north by the end of February. I have to arrange for a replacement here on the key and—"

"You can't leave." Leila finally found her voice. "You love it here."

"Yes, I do love it here. But I *can* leave. And I will. I want to be with you, Leila."

Several people in the crowd began to whistle and applaud and Leila covered her face with her hands. "I can't deal with this."

Marsh took Leila's hand, dragging her toward one of the framed-off doors. He pulled her out of the shell of the house and didn't stop walking until they were on the beach. Alone.

"I'm sorry." He looked tired and unhappy and Leila's heart lurched. "What are you doing out here, anyway? You were supposed to take it easy today."

"I was over at your office looking for you. I ran into Frankie and she brought me over here."

"You were looking for me?" He looked as if he didn't quite believe her.

"I'm not going to marry Elliot. I only told Simon that because he was making me crazy." She was babbling now but unable to stop. "I mean, he had us all neatly paired off and dropped into a slot marked Happily Ever After. And that got me very annoyed—that combined with knowing that we . . . that what we did last night—

which, by the way, was amazingly wonderful. So please don't be mad or hurt or anything because I didn't mean what I said. To Simon," she added. "About Elliot."

"Ah." He glanced out at the sparkling ocean, and when he looked back at her, there was a glint of humor in his eyes. "I'm glad you cleared that up. Except, would you mind repeating the part about Elliot?"

"I'm not going to marry him."

Marsh nodded. "That's what I thought you said. And the part about last night? Something about splendid or wonderful?"

"Amazingly wonderful."

"That was it." Marsh smiled, and gently touched her cheek. "I love Sunrise Key, Leila, but there's nothing for me here if you're a thousand miles away."

"And if I'm not?"

She could see in the warmth of his brown eyes that he was daring to hope. "If I asked you, would you stay?"

Leila kissed him.

This was what it was like to be in love, this feeling of utter desperation and desire, this sensation that a mere kiss was a trip to paradise. And what a kiss it was. Marsh's mouth was soft and warm and tasted so sweet. The world seemed to tilt on its side, off balance and askew. He met her tongue with his own in a sensual dance that released a barrage of intense memories of the night before, when he'd held her, touched her, stroked her, kissed her just like this—and made her irrevocably his own. And Leila knew the answer to his question.

"Yes." She pulled back and gazed into his eyes. "I love you, and I'd like to stay."

Marsh closed his eyes, and when he opened them again, Leila realized he'd been blinking back a sudden rush of tears. "You love me." He stopped to clear his throat. "Enough to marry me? Enough to move back here, back home?"

"Yes." Leila looked at the house going up on the bluff above the water. "But it'll be a new home for me. It'll be yours and mine."

Marsh pulled her into his arms and kissed her again.

"Did she say yes?" someone called down from the construction site.

Marsh didn't lift his head from Leila's sweet lips. But he raised one hand and gave a thumbs-up affirmation.

"She said yes!" the voice cried.

From atop the hill came sounds of cheering and laughter.

"We are going to have one heck of an enormous wedding," Leila heard Millie Waters shout.

And they did.

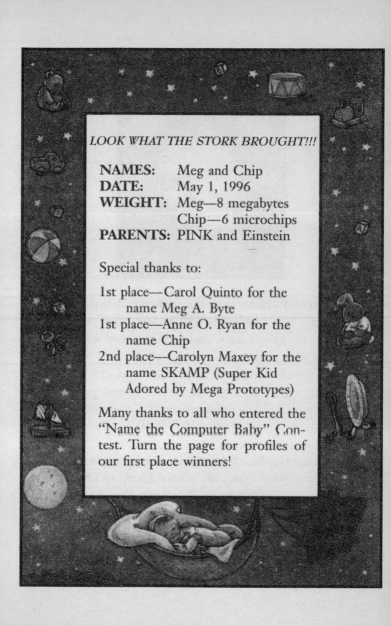

LOOK WHAT THE STORK BROUGHT!!!

NAMES: Meg and Chip
DATE: May 1, 1996
WEIGHT: Meg—8 megabytes
Chip—6 microchips
PARENTS: PINK and Einstein

Special thanks to:

1st place—Carol Quinto for the
name Meg A. Byte
1st place—Anne O. Ryan for the
name Chip
2nd place—Carolyn Maxey for the
name SKAMP (Super Kid
Adored by Mega Prototypes)

Many thanks to all who entered the
"Name the Computer Baby" Contest. Turn the page for profiles of
our first place winners!

Carol Quinto lives in Deltona, Florida, with her husband, Mike, and two psychotic cats. Carol and her husband have been married for twenty years, and are still very much in love. An avid reader and true romantic at heart, Carol particularly likes contemporary romances (Loveswepts, naturally), Patricia Potter historicals, regencies, and mysteries. Fortunately, she shares the same tastes with her mother (who lives next door), so they are able to trade books. Both Carol and her mom are devoted fans of Einstein and PINK, and are thrilled about their new additions!

Anne O. Ryan and her husband of twenty-six years live in DeFuniak Springs, Florida, where they are the proud parents of seven children and four grandsons. Anne is an elementary school teacher, a volunteer for the PTA, Cub Scouts, Boy Scouts, and Little League Soccer, the secretary of the North Walton County Republican Club, and a member of her local Methodist church. Anne also loves to sew, crochet, and travel. And did we mention that Anne loves to read? Well, she does, voraciously, sometimes devouring as many as twenty books a week!

THE EDITORS' CORNER

Next month come celebrate LOVESWEPT's THIRTEENTH ANNIVERSARY with a stellar lineup of your favorite authors, who prove that spooky thirteen, even the more chilling Friday the Thirteenth, can bring the best kind of luck. In each of their novels, the hero and heroine experience unexpected twists and exhilarating turns in their lives—and before they know it, they're swept away into the most passionate journey of all. So put your superstitions aside and join us next month on an exploration of the romantic power of thirteen.

Victoria Leigh casts an irresistible spell in **WAIT FOR MIDNIGHT**, LOVESWEPT #790. He usually draws people to him the way a magnet beckons steel, but attorney Ben Philips has never ached to charm a lady into his life as he does when he spies Kate Hendricks in her hospital flower shop. Stunned by unexpected yearning, Kate meets temptation with a tease—until she discovers Ben's ruthless interest in a mysterious patient she's taken under her wing. Victoria Leigh delivers tenderness and sizzle for a top-notch romantic read.

Praised by *Romantic Times* as "fascinating," the MAC'S ANGELS series by award-winner Sandra Chastain continues with **SINNER AND SAINT**, LOVESWEPT #791. Nikolai Sandor doesn't want to feel anything for the sleeping woman who resembles a fairy-tale princess, but only he can give Karen Miller a reason to live! Murmuring endearments, he tries to convince her they are more than strangers . . . until she awakens and begs her gypsy lover to make her fantasies come true. But can she forgive him for not promising forever? If you're looking for enchantment, then Sandra Chastain's beguiling novel is perfect for you.

Thrilling romance and breathtaking suspense ignite the pages of **PLAYING WITH FIRE**, LOVESWEPT #792, by Debra Dixon. Haunted by a long-ago secret hidden deeper than a dream, Maggie St. John can't brush aside the finger of suspicion arson investigator Beau Grayson points her way. He senses she knows more about the hospital blaze than she's telling him, and he's determined to get the truth—even if it means challenging her to face her tragic past. Summer is about to get hotter with this scorching novel from terrific talent Debra Dixon.

Mary Kay McComas is at her delightful best in **GOT IT BAD**, LOVESWEPT #793. When Dr. Mack McKissack storms the fortress of Kurt Andropov's laboratory to discover what he might be concealing, she doesn't plan on staying any longer than she has to in the devil's lair! Then a shocking accident places her in isolation with the maverick genius, and Mack has to deal not only with the unknown bug that threatens their lives, but also with the fiery attraction arcing between two rivals on the edge. Mary Kay Mc-Comas delivers pure gold with this hilarious, outrageous, and heartwarming romance.

Happy reading!

With warmest wishes,

Beth de Guzman   Shauna Summers
Senior Editor   Editor

P.S. Watch for these Bantam women's fiction titles coming in June: From Jane Feather—the incomparable author of national bestsellers VIOLET and VALENTINE—comes **VICE,** her newest unforgettable romance. Suzanne Robinson takes readers back to the Victorian world of LADY DANGEROUS in **THE ENGAGEMENT,** a mesmerizing love story about a freethinking young woman and a gun-toting Texan. Bestselling author Sandra Canfield, author of DARK JOURNEY, presents a gripping tale as a desperate call from the past throws a man and a woman together again in **NIGHT MOVES**. Finally, from Susan Johnson, the award-winning mistress of sizzling historical romance, comes **SWEET LOVE, SURVIVE**, the powerful conclusion to the bestselling Kuzan Dynasty series begun in SEIZED BY LOVE and LOVE STORM.

Be sure to see next month's LOVESWEPTs for a preview of these exceptional novels. And immediately following this page, preview the Bantam women's fiction titles on sale now!

Don't miss these extraordinary books
by your favorite Bantam authors

On sale in April:

THE UGLY DUCKLING
by Iris Johansen

THE UNLIKELY ANGEL
by Betina Krahn

DANGEROUS TO HOLD
by Elizabeth Thornton

THE REBEL AND THE REDCOAT
by Karyn Monk

New York Times bestselling author of *Lion's Bride*

IRIS JOHANSEN

creates a thrilling world of sinister intrigue and dark desire in her spectacular contemporary hardcover debut

THE UGLY DUCKLING

"Crackling suspense and triumphant romance with a brilliant roller coaster of a plot."   —Julie Garwood

Plain, soft-spoken Nell Calder isn't the type of woman to inspire envy, lust—or murderous passions. Until one night on an exotic island in the Aegean Sea, at an elegant gathering that should have cemented her husband's glorious career in finance, the unimaginable happens . . . and in the space of a heartbeat, Nell's life, her dreams, her future are shattered by a spray of bullets and the razor edge of a blade. Though badly hurt, Nell emerges from the nightmare a woman transformed. Delicate surgery gives her an exquisitely beautiful face. Rehabilitation gives her a strong, lithe body. And Nicholas Tanek, a mysterious stranger who compels both fear and fascination, gives her a reason to go on living: revenge—at any price.

The information was wrong, Nicholas thought in disgust as he gazed down at the surf crashing on the rocks below. No one would want to kill Nell Calder.

If there was a target here, it was probably Kavinski. As head of an emerging Russian state he had the power to be either a cash cow or extremely trouble-some. Nell Calder wouldn't be considered trouble-some to anyone. He had known the answers to all the questions he had asked her but he had wanted to see her reactions. He had been watching her all evening and it was clear she was a nice, shy woman, totally out of her depth even with those fairly innocuous sharks downstairs.

Unless she was more than she appeared. Possibly. She seemed as meek as a lamb but she'd had the guts to toss him out of her daughter's room when she had enough of him.

Still, everyone fought back if the battle was im-portant enough. She hadn't wanted to share her daughter with him. No, the information must mean something else. When he went back downstairs he would stay close to Kavinski.

"Here we go up, up, up
High in the sky so blue.
Here we go down, down, down
Brushing the rose so red."

She was singing to the kid. He had always liked lullabies. There was a sense of warmth and reassur-ance about them that had been missing in his own life. Since the dawn of time mothers had sung to their children and they would probably still be singing to them a thousand years from now.

The song ended with a low chuckle and mur-mured words he couldn't hear.

Nell came out of the bedroom and closed the door a few minutes later. She was flushed and glowing with an expression as soft as melted butter.

"I've never heard that lullaby before," he said.

She looked startled, as if she'd forgotten he was still here. "It's very old. My grandmother used to sing it to me."

"Is Jill asleep?"

"No, but she will be soon. I started the music box for her again. By the time it finishes, she usually nods off."

"She's a beautiful child."

"Yes." A luminous smile turned her plain face radiant. "Yes, she is."

He stared at her, intrigued. He found he wanted to keep that smile on her face. "And bright?"

"Sometimes too bright. Her imagination can be troublesome. But she's always reasonable and you can talk to—" She broke off and her eagerness faded. "But this can't interest you. I forgot the tray. I'll go back for it."

"Don't bother. You'll disturb Jill. The maid can pick it up in the morning."

She gave him a level glance. "That's what I told you."

He smiled. "But then I didn't want to listen. Now it makes perfect sense to me."

"Because it's what you want to do."

"Exactly."

"I have to go back too. I haven't met Kavinski yet." She moved toward the door.

"Wait. I think you'll want to remove that smear of chocolate from the skirt of your gown first."

"Damn." She frowned as she looked down at the stain. "I forgot." She turned toward the bathroom and said dryly, "Go on. I assure you I don't need your help with this problem."

He hesitated.

She glanced at him pointedly over her shoulder.

He had no excuse for staying, not that that small fact would have deterred him.

But he also had no reason. He had been steered wrong. He had lived by his instincts too long not to trust them, and right now they were telling him this woman wasn't a target of any sort. He should be watching Kavinski.

He turned toward the door. "I'll tell the maid you're ready for her to come back."

"Thank you, that's very kind of you," she said automatically as she disappeared into the bathroom.

Good manners obviously instilled from childhood. Loyalty. Gentleness. A nice woman whose world was centered on that sweet kid. He had definitely drawn a blank.

The maid wasn't waiting in the hallway. He'd have to send up one of the servants from downstairs.

He moved quickly through the corridors and started down the staircase.

Shots.

Coming from the ballroom.

Christ.

He tore down the stairs.

She was too good to be true.
He was too bad to resist.

Experience the enchanting wit of
New York Times bestselling
BETINA KRAHN
author of *The Last Bachelor* and
The Perfect Mistress

in the delicious new love story
THE UNLIKELY ANGEL

With her soft heart and angelic face, Madeline Duncan is no one's idea of a hardheaded businesswoman. So when the lovely spinster comes into an unexpected inheritance and uses her newfound wealth to start a business, she causes quite a stir . . . especially with barrister Lord Cole Mandeville, who has been appointed by the courts to keep Madeline from frittering away her fortune. Handsome, worldly, and arrogant, Cole knows just how ruthless the world can be—and that an innocent like Miss Duncan is heading straight for heartbreak, bankruptcy, or worse. But when he sets out to show Madeline the error of her ways, Cole is in for the surprise of his life . . . as he finds himself falling under the spell of a woman who won't believe the worst about anyone—even a jaded rogue like him.

"One of the genre's most creative writers. Her
ingenious romances always entertain and leave
the readers with a warm glow."
—*Romantic Times*

Spellbinding. Intoxicating. Riveting.
Elizabeth Thornton's gift for romance is nothing
less than addictive. Now from this bestselling
author comes her most passionate love story yet.

DANGEROUS TO HOLD

by

ELIZABETH THORNTON

He'd accosted her on a dark London street, sure that she
was his missing wife. But a few moments in her company
assured Marcus Lytton that Miss Catherine Courtnay was
nothing like Catalina. Cool and remote, with a tongue as
tart as a lemon and eyes that could flash with temper, the
fiery-haired beauty was everything his scheming adventur-
ess wife wasn't—innocent, loyal, and honest. And so he
uttered the words that would sweep Catherine into his life,
and into a desperate plan that could spell disaster for them
both: "I want you to play the part of my wife. . . ."

"You are, are you not, my lord, a *married* man?"

The smile was erased. "What do you know of my
wife?" he asked.

She hesitated, shrugged, and said boldly, "Until
tonight, I knew only what everyone else knows, that

you'd married a Spanish girl when you served with Wellington in Spain."

"And after tonight?"

This time she did not falter. "I know that you hate her enough to kill her."

His eyes burned into hers, then the look was gone and the careless smile was in place. "You have misread the situation. It is my wife who wishes to kill me. She may yet succeed. Oh, don't look so stricken. I believe it happens in the best of families. Divorce is so hard to come by, and for a Catholic girl the word doesn't exist." His voice turned hard. "So you see, Catalina and I are bound together until death us do part. An intolerable situation."

Her mind was racing off in every direction. There were a million questions she wanted to ask, but she dared not voice a single one. Even now he was suspicious of her. She could feel it in her bones.

She tried to look amused. "I'm sure, my lord, you are exaggerating."

"Am I? I wonder." His mood changed abruptly. "Enough about me. I am at a disadvantage here. I know nothing about you, and until I know more, I refuse to let you go."

He spoke gaily, as though it were all a great game, but she wasn't taken in by it. She'd seen that darker side of him and knew that the danger wasn't over yet. She intended, if at all possible, to leave this place without his knowing who she was or where to find her.

She moistened her lips. "My lord, I appeal to you as a gentleman to let me go. You see, there is someone waiting for me. If he were to hear of my . . . misadventure, it could prove awkward for me."

There was a strange undercurrent in the silence,

as though her words disturbed him in some way. "I see," he said. "And this gentleman, I take it, is someone you met tonight at Mrs. Spencer's house. Did you make a secret assignation?"

Alarm coursed through her veins. "Mrs. Spencer? I know no one by that name."

"Don't you? I could have sworn that I saw you leave her house tonight. What happened? Did you quarrel? Did she throw you out in those rags? I know how jealous women can be. And you are very beautiful. Did you steal one of her lovers? Is that it? Who is waiting for you? Is it Worcester? Berkeley? Whatever they offered, I can do better."

A moment before, she had been trembling in her shoes. Now a wave of rage flooded through her. Each question was more insulting than the last, and he was doing it on purpose. This time, when she rose to her feet, there was no tremor in her knees. She was Catherine Courtnay and no man spoke to her in those terms. "My business with Mrs. Spencer," she said, "is no concern of yours."

"So, you were there!"

"And if I was?"

There was a moment when she knew she had made that blunder she had tried so hard to avoid. He rose to face her and his eyes glittered brilliantly. Then he reached for her, and hard, muscular arms wrapped around her, dragging her against thighs of iron and a rock-hard chest. She could feel the brass buttons of his coat digging into her. Her arms were trapped at her sides. One hand cupped her neck, then his lips were against her mouth.

From the exciting new voice of

KARYN MONK

author of *Surrender to a Stranger*

THE REBEL AND THE REDCOAT

"Karyn Monk . . . brings the romance of the era to readers with her spellbinding storytelling talents. This is a new author to watch."   —*Romantic Times*

When he saw the lovely young woman struggling with her captor, Damien didn't care which side of the bloody war she was on. He only knew that he had never seen such extraordinary beauty and raw courage in his life. Yet Damien couldn't know that one day this innocent farm girl was destined to betray him. She would become Charles Town's most irresistible spy, dazzling officers with her charms even as she stripped them of strategic secrets. But when a twist of fate brings Josephine back into his life again, Damien will gamble everything on the chance that he can make this exquisite rebel surrender . . . if only in his arms.

Jo stiffened with terror as she lay on the ground and waited for the Indian's blade to carve into her back. Despite her determination not to show her fear, a sob escaped her lips. She was going to die. She waited for her body to be ruthlessly stabbed. The Indian fell heavily onto her, crushing her with his weight, and she screamed, a scream born of utter despair. She had failed. Now Anne and Lucy and Samuel would die. The warrior jerked a few times. Then he let out a sigh and was still. Jo lay frozen beneath him, uncertain what had happened.

Damien dropped his pistol and collapsed against the ground, cursing with every breath he took. He realized his wound was severe, and that he was losing a tremendous amount of blood. He rolled onto his back and vainly tried to stanch the flow with his hands. In a moment or two he would be so weak he would be past the point of caring whether or not he bled to death. It was strange, he mused grimly, but somehow when he had come to the colonies he had not imagined his death would be at the hands of an Indian as he tried to save a simple farm girl.

"Are you all right, Jo?" demanded Samuel anxiously. He moved to where she lay buried beneath the dead warrior.

"I think so," she managed, her voice thin and trembling. "Help me get him off."

Samuel grabbed one of the Indian's arms and pulled. Jo pushed until the dead man's body moved enough for her to scramble out from underneath it. The minute she was free she rushed over to the injured man who had saved her life.

Her throat constricted in horror as she stared down at him. Numbly she took in the scarlet color of his torn jacket, the white waistcoat stained ruby with blood, and the filthy white of his breeches. "Oh dear Lord," she gasped, appalled. "You're a *redcoat*!"

Damien forced his eyes open to look at the woman who had cost him his life. Her eyes were the color of the sky, as clear and brilliant a shade of blue as he had ever seen. Her sunlit hair tumbled wildly over her shoulders, forming a golden veil of silk around her. *It was worth it*, he decided absently as pain clouded over his mind.

She did not move closer but continued to stare at him, her expression a mixture of wariness and fear. He frowned, wondering why she was afraid. And then her words pierced through the dark haze that had almost claimed his consciousness.

Christ, he thought as blackness drowned his senses.

A bloody patriot.

To enter the sweepstakes outlined below, you must respond by the date specified and
follow all entry instructions published elsewhere in this offer.

DREAM COME TRUE SWEEPSTAKES

Sweepstakes begins 9/1/94, ends 1/15/96. To qualify for the Early Bird Prize, entry must be received by the date specified elsewhere in this offer. Winners will be selected in random drawings on 2/29/96 by an independent judging organization whose decisions are final. Early Bird winner will be selected in a separate drawing from among all qualifying entries.

Odds of winning determined by total number of entries received. Distribution not to exceed 300 million.

Estimated maximum retail value of prizes: Grand (1) $25,000 (cash alternative $20,000); First (1) $2,000; Second (1) $750; Third (50) $75; Fourth (1,000) $50; Early Bird (1) $5,000. Total prize value: $86,500.

Automobile and travel trailer must be picked up at a local dealer; all other merchandise prizes will be shipped to winners. Awarding of any prize to a minor will require written permission of parent/guardian. If a trip prize is won by a minor, s/he must be accompanied by parent/legal guardian. Trip prizes subject to availability and must be completed within 12 months of date awarded. Blackout dates may apply. Early Bird trip is on a space available basis and does not include port charges, gratuities, optional shore excursions and onboard personal purchases. Prizes are not transferable or redeemable for cash except as specified. No substitution for prizes except as necessary due to unavailability. Travel trailer and/or automobile license and registration fees are winners' responsibility as are any other incidental expenses not specified herein.

Early Bird Prize may not be offered in some presentations of this sweepstakes. Grand through third prize winners will have the option of selecting any prize offered at level won. All prizes will be awarded. Drawing will be held at 204 Center Square Road, Bridgeport, NJ 08014. Winners need not be present. For winners list (available in June, 1996), send a self-addressed, stamped envelope by 1/15/96 to: Dream Come True Winners, P.O. Box 572, Gibbstown, NJ 08027.

THE FOLLOWING APPLIES TO THE SWEEPSTAKES ABOVE:

No purchase necessary. No photocopied or mechanically reproduced entries will be accepted. Not responsible for lost, late, misdirected, damaged, incomplete, illegible, or postage-die mail. Entries become the property of sponsors and will not be returned.

Winner(s) will be notified by mail. Winner(s) may be required to sign and return an affidavit of eligibility/release within 14 days of date on notification or an alternate may be selected. Except where prohibited by law, entry constitutes permission to use of winners' names, hometowns, and likenesses for publicity without additional compensation. Void where prohibited or restricted. All federal, state, provincial, and local laws and regulations apply.

All prize values are in U.S. currency. Presentation of prizes may vary; values at a given prize level will be approximately the same. All taxes are winners' responsibility.

Canadian residents, in order to win, must first correctly answer a time-limited skill testing question administered by mail. Any litigation regarding the conduct and awarding of a prize in this publicity contest by a resident of the province of Quebec may be submitted to the Regie des loteries et courses du Quebec.

Sweepstakes is open to legal residents of the U.S., Canada, and Europe (in those areas where made available) who have received this offer.

Sweepstakes in sponsored by Ventura Associates, 1211 Avenue of the Americas, New York, NY 10036 and presented by independent businesses. Employees of these, their advertising agencies and promotional companies involved in this promotion, and their immediate families, agents, successors, and assignees shall be ineligible to participate in the promotion and shall not be eligible for any prizes covered herein.   SWP 3/95